Reincarnated by Magic

Thorne Sisters Chronicles
Book Two

RENEE JOINER

Oshun
Publications

Contents

Reincarnated by Magic Copyright © 2020 by Renee Joiner
ISBN: 978-1-950378-08-1

Book Design by MMB
Published by Oshun Publications
www.oshunpublications.com

Other Books by Renee

Thorne Sisters Chronicles
Possessed by Magic

Did you know you can take every story with you?

I know it's tough these days to simply find the time to relax and curl up with a good book. This is why I'm delighted to share that I have books available in audio book format.

Best of all, you can get the audio book version of any book by me for free as part of a 30-day Audible trial.

Members get free audio books every month and exclusive discounts. It's an excellent way to explore and determine if audio book learning works for you.

If you're not satisfied, you can cancel anytime within the trial period. You won't be charged, and you can even keep your audio book.

To choose a free audio book, click on your favorite title's cover to be taken to Audible's website for details.

Remember, there's no obligation to buy.

reneejoinerauthor.com/audiobooks

JOIN MY NEWSLETTER

GET UPDATES, FREEBIES & GIVEAWAYS

RENEEJOINERAUTHOR.COM/NEWSLETTER

Chapter One

THE CROW STOOD ON THE LEDGE JUST OUTSIDE THE window and looked her straight in the eyes. Rayven leveled its gaze, sure that in just a few seconds, it would dissipate into a puff of smoke as black as its eyes.

It didn't, though. It remained, perched on the concrete slab that jutted out four floors above the gray courtyard below, and then instead of disappearing, it flapped its wings just once and was airborne. Rayven tracked it with her eyes as it sailed on the currents of air and found a perch on the brittle branches of the courtyard's solitary tree.

It is real. The crow is real, Rayven thought excitedly, and she no longer saw things that weren't really there.

The rest of the courtyard was bleak and lifeless. There was a rickety wooden bench that Rayven didn't think she had seen anyone sit on in all the time she had been there. She wondered if it would even support anyone's weight, as old as it looked. She would think it would be for visitors, but she hadn't seen any of those while there either.

"Staring at birds again?" Rayven didn't need to see his

1

face to know it was Harvey. His aftershave announced his presence the minute he left his room down the hall. It was something that aged him, as well. It smelled like Old Spice, and Rayven was pretty sure they didn't even make that anymore. She could picture Harvey hoarding a bathroom cabinet full of the stuff just because he didn't want to use anything else.

"At least they're flying away now, and not disappearing into a puff of smoke like before." She kept her eye on the bird for just a moment longer, making sure she wasn't talking too soon, before turning to face the man.

"Well, that is progress, I guess." His chuckle clucked in his throat, and Rayven wondered if she would miss the sound when she got out of there.

Harvey lowered himself into the seat next to her. The couches in the recreation room were not the kind that envelope you and invites you to stay awhile or have a nap. They were quite clearly selected for their sturdiness. Heavy enough that they couldn't be lifted by a patient on a manic spree and hard enough that you wouldn't consider sleeping off your sedatives on them.

The rest of the furniture was just as functional, and for the first time, Rayven wondered why they even called it a recreation area. There was nothing recreational about it.

It was only another area to herd people into when you didn't want them in their rooms. The staff claimed that it was important for patients to spend at least part of their day outside their rooms.

Rayven preferred the recreation room on most days, but there were also days when she just wanted to curl up in her bed and stay there. She guessed that it wasn't too different from being on the outside. You have your good days and your bad days, whether you are in an institution or not. Rayven had laughed the first time she had heard the term 'mental health day' as a reference to someone taking time off from the world to take care of their emotional state. She wondered if they could use that term in Grand Meadow. She turned her attention back to Harvey as he spoke. "Do you think that means you're getting better, then?"

It took a while for Rayven to realize that Harvey was talking to her, and she studied his face before replying, considering what the correct response would be. Although his short clipped hair was now closer to white than the chestnut it once was, his mustache hadn't aged as quickly, so it sat like a chocolate slug on his upper lip. The slug did a jig every time he talked, and it often took all of Rayven's might not to laugh out loud at the spectacle.

It was neatly trimmed, though, which was strange in itself, considering they didn't have access to scissors. Harvey's eyes were slightly bloodshot, a remnant of a life-time of rough nights, perhaps. They all knew so little about each other that for all, Rayven knew the old man could have been a raging alcoholic before he came there.

"I don't know Harv, I think so. I haven't seen anything... that's...well, you know." Rayven smiled faintly and picked at a piece of lint on her uniform leg. The blue scrubs were issued to her on the day she arrived, and although a fresh pair appeared daily, folded up in a neat stack on her bed when she returned from breakfast, they were always well worn and the same style. They looked exactly like what surgeons wore to operate in, and Rayven had thought that odd in the beginning.

"Not really there?" Harvey guffawed now, letting his chuckle erupt and throwing his head back. Rayven smiled, understanding that in Grand Meadow, it was necessary to be able to laugh at herself. Your sanity depended on it. The terror that came with not having control of your own mind was briefly forgotten when you could find humor in your own pain.

"Quiet down, Harvey!" The voice came from the opposite end of the recreation room, and someone who had never met the ex-school teacher, Maude, would be forgiven for thinking she was in charge at Grand Meadow. Until Rayven had understood Maude's particular malady, she had honestly thought the woman had been a nurse there.

On a good day, Maude realized that she had left her 30 year teaching career behind when her delusions had taken her over. Still, on a bad day, she was sure that all the patients at Grand Meadow were her school charges, and she was tasked with keeping them in line.

"Okay, Maude. Sorry about that." Harvey rolled his eyes in Rayven's direction. Seemingly forgetting that his own occasional delusions around whether he still owned a ranch or not also reared their head on occasion.

"You know when you first arrived here, you reminded me so much of my granddaughter that it was painful to look at you."

His revelation hit Rayven hard, and she was suddenly unsure whether he said it or she imagined it. She looked at Harvey, and there was a small tear in the corner of his eye. He blinked it away and, with it, the topic of conversation.

She suddenly realized what a strange situation she was in.

Stuck in this building with all these people. People who were at the lowest point in their lives, and yet, they didn't know each other at all. The conversations they had in the recreation room were mostly about dull things; television programs or favorite foods.

On occasion, the gossip would turn to who had experienced an episode in the last few days and had to be sedated. They never discussed their lives, their loved ones, or their pain.

Sometimes Rayven wondered if they were really human at all. Yes, she even questioned if she was human. The medication they gave them made her feel hollow. When she had her episodes, Rayven felt as though she was losing her mind, so in all, she felt like an empty, insane alien at the best of times.

Things had been better recently, though. Something had changed inside her. She couldn't place her finger on it, but, at the very least, she hadn't had any weird visions in a very long time. Her attention was drawn back to Harvey and the pain he had just shared with her.

"Right then," he stood to attention, "it's time for my afternoon nap, lass." He winked at her and then turned on his heel, likely not realizing that it was 10 am.

Rayven considered her own state of mind for a moment. It had been a long time since she felt like she belonged at Grand Meadow. She felt a tiny trickle of trepidation and pushed it down. No. It wouldn't be like the last time.

She had felt this way before. Like she was better and ready to leave, but Dr. Hewitt had shown her that she was wrong.

She thanked the heavens for Dr. Hewitt every day. If it wasn't for him, Rayven would still be living in two worlds, unsure of which was real and often hoping both were illusions. He had helped her through, and now she could make him proud by telling him that she was ready to go home.

Right now, Rayven was sure she was living in reality now, in the one world that mattered. Dr. Hewitt had explained that sometimes the mind split, taking one part of it one way and the other in another direction. His job, he had said, was to help her bring those two parts back together so that she could be whole again.

The recreation room was almost empty, Rayven realized. Today must be a bad day for a lot of patients on the 5th floor of Grand Meadow. It seemed as though everyone except her and Maude was having their afternoon naps at 10 am.

As she stood, Maude's head shot up from her knitting. Without missing a beat, Rayven asked the question, "May I have a hall pass, Teacher Maude?" She had learned to play along with the other patient's delusions.

Not everyone was going to get better, like her, and some of the patients would be here forever, fighting their failing minds. It was easier to be kind than to fight their insanity. That sort of attitude almost always ended badly.

Maude's face crinkled.

"Are you mad, child?"

Her delusion was gone, and Rayven looked like a fool. She smiled at the old lady.

"It appears I am, Ms. Maude. Mad as a hatter apparently." She strode out of the recreation room, shaking her head. If you weren't slightly touched when you arrived at Grand Meadow, you might just be completely insane when you left. She wondered how long term staff like Dr. Hewitt kept their sanity. Admittedly, working with people who lived in a different dimension every day took its toll on you? Dr. Hewitt seemed just fine, though. Even more than that, he was one of the kindest, most calm people that Rayven had ever met. He made her feel better every time she saw him. She had no doubt that she would miss seeing him. She wondered, for a moment, if Grand Meadow did an outpatient service. Then she could come back and still see Dr. Hewitt, but she wouldn't have to live there.

The 5th floor was relatively open to patients. No one

there was really dangerous unless they were in a mania or delusion, and then they were kept in their rooms anyway. The only place that the patients couldn't enter without permission was Dr. Hewitt's office. Rayven's sneakers squeaked on the highly polished floor as she made her way to the reception area. The staff roster was displayed so that everyone could see which orderlies and doctors were working that day. Each floor had its own team based on the needs of the patients. The more violent patients and those who had been hospitalized by court order were on the upper floors. The running joke among Grand Meadow residents was that the higher you go in the building, the higher you get. A bad wordplay on the types of medications given to the more violent patients. The elevator could be accessed only by the fingerprint of an authorized staff member. There was a ghost story of sorts that patients told amongst themselves when the staff was out of earshot. The story went that on one of the upper floors of Grand Meadow; they didn't have fingerprint recognition anymore because a patient had cut off a doctor's finger to escape the building. On that floor, it was alleged that they had a security guard that had to buzz you through. Rayven had actually laughed when she had heard the story for the first time. It just sounded ridiculous.

The more paranoid patients had not taken kindly to her laughing. She soon learned to pretend that she took everything seriously unless one of the others laughed first. Such was life at Grand Meadow, and that was precisely why Rayven was so desperate to prove that she was better and could leave. She truly feared that if she stayed there much longer, she might never be fit to leave.

Rayven ran her finger down the list of staff members, stopping at Dr. Hewitt. According to the roster, he would be in later that afternoon.

"Looking for me?" Rayven spun around to face the voice. Caleb stood inches from her, and a butterfly batted its wings in her stomach.

She laughed nervously. "Uh...no, actually, I wanted to see if Dr. Hewitt would be in today." Rayven couldn't be sure, but she thought a shadow passed over Caleb's face. Disappointment?

"Oh, right. Anything wrong? I mean, you look great." He stumbled a little over his words, but his broad smile made up for it. "What I mean is you look healthy." He emphasized the last word to assure her that his statement was entirely professional.

Caleb had noticed that Rayven had been coping progressively better, especially over the last few weeks. His first day as an intern at Grand Meadow had been a few days after she had been brought in. To say that she had been a mess was an understatement. Her auburn hair had been matted with sweat, and he had longed to gently brush it out so that she would feel better. Her eyes had reminded him of a feral cat that had been brought into the animal shelter he sometimes volunteered at. The color was almost identical, an amber hue he had rarely seen. Still, it was the way they darted back and forth and then, at times, stared unseeing at some invisible horror in her mind's eye, which made his heart break for her. As he had watched over her, though, she had grown steadily stronger. As she smiled at him now, her hair neatly pulled back into a ponytail that only accentuated her youth, she appeared almost whole again. At 21, she was one of the youngest patients there and the closest to his age. Seeing her there, especially in her early days of confusion and terror, had made him grateful that his own life had turned out the way it had. If working at Grand Meadow had taught him anything, it was that it was only a single stroke of luck that decided whether you would be the patient or the doctor.

"There's nothing wrong at all. In fact," she looked as though she were about to reveal a secret, "I think I'm ready to go home." Rayven hadn't expected the huge gasp of air Caleb had taken in, and she thought his lungs might explode if he held it in any longer. "That's why I want to see Dr. Hewitt. To tell him."

Caleb was looking around the reception, as though to see who else was present. The elderly receptionist, Mrs. Brindle, had likely not heard a word that had been uttered. She was engrossed in a book she was reading.

Rayven had glimpsed the cover, and the bare chested man on the front with the golden skinned Amazonian beauty made Rayven think that it was probably not entirely proper reading for the workplace. The woman had worked at Grand Meadow for so long, though, she could perhaps bring a real life bare chested man into reception, and no one would notice. To say she was part of the furniture didn't quite cut it. She was more like part of the wallpaper. "That is amazing news, Rayven." Caleb's voice was low. "Seriously, I'm really happy for you." He sounded anything but happy.

Rayven was a little taken aback by his response. If she were honest, she had expected a bit more excitement and a little less apprehension. She wondered whether he would miss her. They had become friendly, and Caleb always had great advice. She had never asked him how old he was but figured that he was probably only a few years older than her. Rayven allowed herself a brief moment to consider that she might see him on the outside, and then, as quickly as the picture had entered her head, she shoved it back down. No, when she walked out the doors of Grand Meadow, she would leave everything behind and go out into her new life with no attachments. That included Caleb. Even her previous thought of being an outpatient was actually ludicrous. There was nothing here for her. She had come here to heal, and she had done just that, in her opinion. That was the end of it.

"So should I give him the message for you? Dr. Hewitt, I mean...that you have something to speak to him about?"

"No!" The word was a little more forceful than she'd intended. She wanted to tell him herself. She had earned that, and Caleb's reticence to her announcement concerned her. She didn't want to risk him telling Dr. Hewitt that he didn't think she was ready. "Sorry, I just mean I would rather talk to him myself about it. Thanks, though." Caleb didn't seem deflated at all by her response.

"Oh, sure. Of course, no problem." He smiled widely again. His smile always reached his eyes. That was one thing that Rayven looked for in people. If your smile doesn't reach your eyes, you're hiding something. Someone had taught her that when she was a child, but she couldn't remember who anymore. "Okay, well, I'm going to get on with it, and I'll see you later?" He started to walk away and then turned back. "Oh, Rayven, I really am happy for you." She wasn't really sure that he was.

"Thank you, Caleb. I appreciate that." She watched him squeak his way down the hallway until he disappeared into the recreation room. She wasn't sure why she felt that he wasn't getting ready to say goodbye in the same way that she was.

"Mrs. Brindle." The woman didn't look up. "I would like to see Dr. Hewitt when he arrives, please. Could you let him know?" Her eyes stayed on her book. Rayven waited. "Mrs....," a single finger shot up. Wait. Okay, I'll wait, Rayven thought.

The old woman searched the counter for her bookmark, placed it between the pages, and put her book squarely on the desk in front of her. The bare chested goliath stared up at Rayven with a look in his eyes that gave her the creeps. Mrs. Brindle looked up.

"Do you have an appointment?" Rayven wondered whether she had actually verbalized the words that she thought she had. The woman's response said that she hadn't.

"Um, I thought that was what I was doing right now? You know, making an appointment?" Her tone was more sarcastic than intended.

"No need to get rude, young lady. You can't make an appointment with me." She started to pick up her book again. "You have to make it with Dr. Hewitt. Only he knows his schedule. I'm not his secretary, you know."

"Okay, but I can't make an appointment if I don't know when he is here, so could you let me know when he is here?"

Rayven shoved her hands down into her pockets to stop herself from snatching the book out of the woman's hands and sending Goliath and his Amazonian woman on a one way flight across the reception area.

"Yes, if I see him." Rayven sighed softly and turned to leave. There was little chance the woman would see a 10 foot blue cow doing a jig in the reception with her head buried in that book.

"Thanks." She muttered as she walked away, reminding herself that Grand Meadow was not the place to be thinking about 10 foot unnaturally colored farm animals. In the outside world, it would be funny. Here you risked a citation for hallucinations, and she wished she was joking. Rayven headed for the recreation room. If Mrs. Brindle actually did call her over the intercom system to announce Dr. Hewitt's arrival, she wanted to be sure to hear her. The patient's rooms had thick steel doors that reminded Rayven of safe doors or the type fitted to bomb shelters. They were entirely soundproof. Although each room was equipped with baby monitors so that staff could hear if any of the patients were in trouble during the night, the sound obviously only went one way, so once that door was closed. There was no way you could hear what was going on outside. When one of the other patients had an episode, Rayven was glad she couldn't hear anything. Still, it was also impossible to know when someone was approaching your room until the access card monitor beeped. It made changing clothes a quick adventure, but she didn't do much of that anyway. Their blue scrubs were worn throughout the day, slept in, and then changed for new scrubs in the morning, and that usually happened when she showered.

Harvey had finished his afternoon/morning nap and was sitting in the chair Rayven had been in earlier.

"Who's staring out the window now?" She joked, hoping he had cheered up a little. He gave her a half smile, only the sadness reached his eyes.

"I think you might be more like my granddaughter than I thought. It's not just the way you look." His face was earnest now, as though he had something significant to tell her. "You know that everything is not always what it appears to be? That's one thing I've learned in my life." Rayven had absolutely no idea what he was talking about, and her expression showed it, so he continued. "My granddaughter used to...see stuff too." Harvey wasn't looking at Rayven anymore. He stared at his clasped hands in his lap instead.

"She was sick too?" Rayven tried. Harvey shook his head slowly, still not making eye contact.

"She wasn't sick, Rayven. It was..." he shrugged his

shoulders, "something else." She was starting to wonder if he had slipped back into a delusion again. "I know it sounds crazy, but there was something special about her, and her visions were part of that. They told her when bad things were going to happen." The older man's voice was so low that Rayven could barely hear him. "She knew that she was going to have the accident that killed her because she saw it happen." Rayven had known that Harvey had lost family, but she didn't realize that it was his grand-daughter. The rest of his statement made very little sense, though. How could she possibly have seen it happen? Her incredulity must have leaked out onto her face as he looked at her. "Look, you don't have to believe me, Rayven, but I know that there was something different about her, and I see it in you, too."

"Hey Harvey, you having a rough day today?" Caleb appeared out of nowhere, and he had one of the orderlies with him. The large man stood a few steps behind, trying not to look as imposing as he naturally did. There was no doubt that he was there for one reason. To control Harvey if the need arose. The orderly's hand twitched at his pocket, and Rayven was sure there was a syringe inside, filled with blue liquid and ready to sedate whoever needed it. Rayven had passed the staff changing rooms one day when the door had just been opened widely, and although it had started swinging shut, it was on a spring, so it took a while.

It had been long enough for Rayven to see the orderlies getting ready for their shift. They had already put their white scrubs on, which differentiated them from the patients. As Rayven watched, they all lined up and drew a syringe of blue fluid from a vial, placed a protective cap over the needle, and slipped it into their pockets. From that day, she watched whenever an orderly's hand went to that pocket. Harvey stood suddenly, and the syringe hand twitched again.

"No, I'm fine. I'm just having a chat with Rayven here. I don't see why you need to come and interrupt us. There's nothing wrong with talking, is there?" Harvey's voice escalated in both volume and annoyance with each word. Rayven moved back in her seat. You don't ever want to get caught between an orderly and a patient when the syringe comes out.

"Okay, Harv, it's all good. I'm just checking on you. Making sure you're okay." Caleb's tone was conciliatory. The way you speak to a child in the throes of a tantrum. He put his hand on Harvey's shoulder, probably to calm him more than anything, else but Harvey exploded.

"Take your hands off me!" He struck out and backed against the window. Rayven pulled her legs up onto the chair, her knees against her chest, in a protective stance. "Can't a person have a conversation? I'm just talking, that's all!" His eyes were wild, and then in a split second, they deadened. The orderly moved quickly for a large man. He had closed in on Harvey and sunk the needle into his arm, straight through his long sleeved shirt, before anyone else knew what was happening. Rayven watched as Harvey sunk to the floor, supported by Caleb and the orderly. Just before he lost consciousness, he managed, "Don't trust them, Rayven."

Rayven was shaking by the time the orderly wheeled Harvey away in a wheelchair, and Caleb sat down next to her.

"Hey, it's okay. I could see he was having a bad day. He just needs to rest. Maybe Dr. Hewitt can adjust his meds when he gets in." Rayven nodded silently. It never got easier. The take downs happened at least once a week. It was usually the same patients, and it had only ever happened to Rayven once, that she knew of. Still, every time someone else went into that state, it was terrifying. "What on earth was he saying to you? I saw the expression on your face. You looked like he was really scaring you."

"No, no, he wasn't scaring me." She felt the need to defend Harvey in his absence. He had clearly suffered a lot of pain in his life, and it was coming out now. "He was talking about his granddaughter." Caleb's face darkened. "What happened to her, Caleb? He said there was an accident."

"I don't know much about it." He inhaled deeply. "It wasn't just her, though. It was the whole family." Rayven's hand was over her mouth to block the horror. "Harvey's son, his daughter-in-law and their two children, Harvey's grandchildren, were killed in the accident. A truck plowed into their car if I remember correctly."

"Poor Harvey! How do you even come back from that?" Rayven asked no one in particular. Caleb answered, anyway.

"Well, people cope with even worse than that, but Harvey couldn't because he was already sick. That's what landed him at Grand Meadow."

Rayven had never given much thought to why some of the patients in Grand Meadow were there. She wasn't sure why, but she had probably just assumed that they had just suddenly started seeing things that weren't there or having visions or manias. She felt a little silly having never considered the fact that some of these people had experienced traumatic things that had been the spark for their downward spiral. Like Harvey. Although Caleb had said that some people can deal with their entire family being wiped out, Rayven couldn't imagine that being true.

"What else did he say to you?" Caleb asked. Rayven had no idea if she could even repeat Harvey's words.

That's how strange they were. She also couldn't shake the feeling that she wasn't supposed to share that part.

"Nothing. Just that I reminded him of her."

"How so?" He barked. Rayven frowned. Where did that come from? "Sorry, I...I'm just concerned about him and mostly you. You're so close to getting out of here. I don't want you to have any setbacks."

"I'm not going to have any setbacks, Caleb. I'm fine, really." Rayven stood, effectively ending the conversation. "I'm going to see if Dr. Hewitt is in yet."

Caleb wondered if she could see his heart pounding through his shirt. It sure felt like she could. That was too close. Far too close for comfort. He would have to watch her more closely, but she was going to Dr. Hewitt's office now, and he couldn't control what happened in there. He listened to her shoes squeak down the corridor until he could hear them no longer. There was no time to waste. Things were happening much faster than he had planned, and he wasn't ready. That really didn't matter, though, because when the time came, he would have to make his move regardless of whether he was ready. The consequences of not getting the job done were more far reaching than anyone could imagine.

Chapter Two

RAYVEN HAD RAISED HER HAND TO KNOCK ON DR. Hewitt's door, but it swung open before her knuckles touched the mahogany.

"Rayven!" Dr. Hewitt's kind face immediately set Rayven's mind at ease. He had that way about him. "So lovely to see you, it's been too long since we last chatted. Do come in." He stood aside and waved his hand in the direction of the high back chairs at the round glass table in his office. Rayven had never seen a psychiatrist before Dr. Hewitt. She expected what you see in the movies. The long, dark couch that patients are intended to relax on, encouraging them to release all of their darkest secrets. Dr. Hewitt's office looked more like a doctor you would go to if you had the flu.

His desk stood in one corner, but it was so small that with his laptop on it, there was barely space for a coffee cup. There was no chair on the opposite side of that table because that wasn't where he spoke to patients. That activity was conducted at the round glass table with the high back chairs around it. The part that made Rayven think about a typical doctor's office was the hospital bed in the corner. It was closed off by sliding curtains, but she had peeked behind there once when Dr. Hewitt had left her alone for a second.

At the time, she had thought it was a bit of an odd thing to have in a psychiatrist's office. It's not like he was taking your blood pressure or using those horrendous lollipop sticks that made you gag, to check your throat for strep. After seeing Harvey carted off, though, as Rayven sat down in one of the high back chairs, she realized that it might be to transport sedated patients. She wondered whether any patients went into manias or delusions in Dr. Hewitt's office and had to be taken down. It was entirely possible. After all, the whole point of being in there was to dig into your psyche.

"So how are you doing? I heard Harvey had a bit of an episode earlier." Dr. Hewitt pushed his office door closed and then turned the key in the lock. Rayven felt a tingle down her spine. Had he done that before? It would make sense that he wouldn't want a session interrupted, but why did that sound frighten her so much? How on earth had he heard about Harvey so fast? Bad news travels fast, Rayven guessed. Dr. Hewitt laughed at her surprise. "I was standing in reception when I heard the shouting. I followed him and the orderly to his room to ensure he got settled. He's resting now."

"Oh good, I'm glad. He was very...upset." She realized that she had taken to using the terminology that the staff employed. They used words like upset, unsettled, or unwell to describe fits of rage, mania, and delusion that would be better described by stronger words. Still, it downplayed the seriousness in a way. Rayven wasn't sure if that was a good thing.

"I saw you sitting with Caleb afterward. Was he able to

comfort you?" I saw you. Was there a hint of accusation in there? Her spine tingled again. She had, on more than one occasion, gotten the impression that Caleb and Dr. Hewitt did not see eye to eye. It wasn't something either of them had said, it was merely a feeling she got.

"Yes. Well, actually, I was fine. I didn't need any comfort." One of Dr. Hewitt's eyebrows shot up, and she realized she sounded a bit like a petulant child. "Sorry, I just... I wanted to chat with you about something, Dr. Hewitt, and it's rather important." The unsaid phrase was: so if we could stop talking about everyone else, which would be great.

"Okay, what would you like to chat about?" Dr. Hewitt leaned back in his chair and folded his hands behind his head. He was one of those people whose age you couldn't really pin down. If Rayven was forced to guess, she would say 55, but he had much less gray hair than Harvey. In fact, it was almost entirely jet black. As black as a crow, she had seen this morning. Crows are bad luck. More spine tingling. Despite the lack of gray hair, his wrinkles gave away that he was a bit older. The skin around his eyes creased into a fan when he smiled.

"I think I'm ready to go home." Rayven blurted it out. She wanted the idea outside of her, maybe then it would feel more realistic. Home. Tingle.

Chapter Three

"You think you are ready to go home." His tone was flat. He wasn't questioning it or saying it with disdain. He simply repeated precisely what she had said.

"Yes. I'm really feeling much better, Dr. Hewitt. I have made a lot of progress. I think that I will cope well at home. I really want to get back to my life."

"Your life?" His repetitions were starting to annoy her. Her spine was now tingling halfway up her back.

"Yes, my life Dr. Hewitt, you know the thing that I left behind when I came to Grand Meadow?" Rayven respected Dr. Hewitt, and she didn't want to be rude to him. In fact, she didn't know why she was being so short tempered with people all of a sudden. It was absolutely out of character for her. Dr. Hewitt was unperturbed. He had dealt with far worse than an annoyed young woman before.

"Well, let's address what brought you in here in the first place." He shifted in his seat and smiled. Gold tooth cap. Rayven could not believe that she hadn't noticed it before. The tingle was now a pounding fist on her spine.

Her forehead started to glisten. "You were having quite disruptive hallucinations when you came in. You called them visions. Do you feel like that is under control now?" Hallucinations. Visions. The pounding fist was at her neck now, and Dr. Hewitt was just looking at her. Waiting for an answer. "Rayven?" The fist pounded her head. Rayven.

Dr. Hewitt's eyes lit up. Flames licked his ears, and his face started to melt. His gold tooth began to liquefy and trickle down his chin, but his mouth was still moving. Help me, Rayven. Help me. Rayven. Rayven. The pounding was so loud that Rayven could barely hear. She dug her fingernails into the arms of the high back chair, forcing herself to hold on to reality as it slowly trickled away like the dribble of liquefied gold down her doctor's chin.

"I can see something is wrong, Rayven. What is it?" Rayven's brow was now dry, and she focused on how she was coming across to Dr. Hewitt. She couldn't let him know that she had just had the beginnings of another vision. He would never allow her to leave Grand Meadow if he knew. She just had to maintain a semblance of normalcy for long enough to convince him that she was okay. She was terrified to be experiencing visions again and bitterly disappointed. She had really thought that every-thing was getting better and that she would soon be living back in the real world.

"Dr. Hewitt, I just think I'm coming down with a bit of a cold. Really, I'm fine." His eyes searched her face for the truth.

"When was the last time you experienced an episode, Rayven?" She wondered if the accusatory tone she heard was just her own guilty conscience. She of all people knew that if she was still having visions, going home was not a great idea, but she really could not stand the thought of much more time at Grand Meadow. The idea so repulsed her that she was willing to lie if that is what it took.

"Weeks ago, Dr. Hewitt, and it really wasn't even that bad. I haven't had a truly bad one in months." She bit the inside of her lip. She really did not want to be lying to him after all that he had done for her. Yet she had to get out of there. Rayven's greatest fear was that if she didn't leave Grand Meadow soon, she never would. Dr. Hewitt stood up and walked over to his desk. He switched on his laptop and started to tap at the keys. Tap tap tap. Tap tap tap. Her spine thumped.

Rayven stood up and opened the office door to see who was knocking. As she turned the handle, she realized she hadn't unlocked it. She knew Dr. Hewitt had locked it, so why was it now unlocked? Tap tap tap. She cracked the door and peered through, unsure why she didn't just open it all the way. A young girl stood at the door. Rayven immediately noticed that she looked very similar to her, auburn hair, amber eyes. The girl was silent. She looked at Rayven imploringly. Who was she? A new patient? She seemed very young to be on the 5th floor, but then Rayven was there too, so perhaps age was not a great grading system for madness. The girl was so familiar to Rayven. Where had she seen her before? Maybe when she arrived? Or perhaps she had seen her in the courtyard? Neither of those options sounded right, though. It was more profound than that. She didn't just know of this girl, she knew her inside and out.

"Hello, can I help you?"

Tap tap tap. Who was knocking now, and where? She'd opened the door, so where was the tapping coming from? Rayven glanced over her shoulder at Dr. Hewitt. He wasn't at his computer anymore. She spun around the room. It was empty. Where was Dr. Hewitt? She looked out the door again, and the girl was gone too. She felt a hand on her arm.

"Rayven, what's happening?" It was Dr. Hewitt's voice.

"There's a girl at the door, Dr. Hewitt. I think she's a patient."

"What girl, Rayven?"

Tap tap tap. Dr. Hewitt was back at his computer.

"I'm just reviewing your medication. If we release you, you will need to continue with your medication, or you may relapse. If you relapse, you will have to immediately be readmitted, and your second stay may be far longer than your first." Rayven watched him typing, wondering how he had gotten back in the room. She had just been standing at the door. He couldn't have left or come back in without her seeing. Had he been behind the sliding curtain that surrounded the hospital bed in the corner? Why would he be? Tap tap tap.

"Rayven. Don't let them give you the drugs." The girl's voice was so soft that Rayven almost hadn't heard her. She was at the round table with her now, although Rayven hadn't heard the door open or close, and Dr. Hewitt hadn't acknowledged the girl's presence. Rayven slowly turned her head and met the girl's gaze. It was like looking into her own eyes. A lone tear rose in the corner of the girl's eye. It started to roll down her cheek, and Rayven felt her own cheek become moist, too. She wiped away a tear, and so did the girl. It was like looking at a mirror image of herself. The girl looked slightly different from her. She wore her hair differently. Her skin was not near as pale as hers had become from being confined for so long.

"Who are you?" Her voice trembled.

"Don't let them give you the drugs, Rayven. Please, you must listen to me." The girl was gripping the sides of the table now, and Rayven could feel it lifting slightly. She was so tiny, how could she be lifting the plate glass table?

"Rayven, are you listening to me?"

"Yes! Stop! Why are you doing this?"

The girl stood up, and suddenly she was as tall as Dr. Hewitt. She gripped the edges of the table and shoved it toward Rayven. "You do not see what is there!" The table flipped, and Rayven shielded her face from what she knew was coming.

The shatter of glass. Silence. Tap tap tap.

"Rayven, you're bleeding!" Dr. Hewitt sounded terrified. She had never heard him sound scared of anything. "How did you turn that table over? It weighs more than both of us!" Rayven blinked away something wet in her eyes. Was she still crying? Through a red haze, she could see Dr. Hewitt standing over her as she lay on the floor. The color had entirely left his face. He was touching her head, and she suddenly realized that the wet, red haze was blood. Where was the girl? Rayven pushed herself up and scanned the room.

"It was the girl! Where is she?"

"What girl, Rayven? There's no one here. Just you and me." Dr. Hewitt placed his hand on her shoulder and tried to get her to lie down again. "Just relax; I'm going to get a doctor. That table hit you hard; you could have a head injury." His hand on her shoulder was like a hundred knives. She screamed in pain and watched as Dr. Hewitt's face morphed into the girl's and then back again. He was her! She was him! "Get off me! Get away from me!" She pushed at Dr. Hewitt, and as he stumbled back, she pushed herself against the wall, bringing her knees up to her chest in protection.

Dr. Hewitt, keeping his eyes on her and his hands

raised so that she could see them, slowly moved toward the curtained cubicle in the corner.

"Rayven, just stay calm," He held his hands out as he backed away from her, attempting to seem less threatening. "I'm going to help you, okay? Let's just get something to help you calm down." Rayven could hear him rattling bottles around behind the curtain. Don't let them give you the drugs, Rayven.

Dr. Hewitt heard the door slam behind Rayven as she made her escape. She slid into the recreation room, breathless and bleeding. An orderly spotted her and gave chase. She had nowhere to go, she knew this, but her legs wouldn't stop moving. She had to avoid letting them give her the drugs. The last thing she remembered was seeing the laundry chute and considering throwing herself down it. A muscled arm wrapped itself around her neck, and a man's voice instructed her not to struggle. She felt a burning sensation in her arm and then...silence, darkness, nothingness.

Chapter Four

THE GIRL WAS SITTING NEXT TO HARVEY. HE HAD HIS ARM around her. They were chuckling and chatting like old friends. Rayven tried to push away the fog that surrounded her so that she could see more clearly, but it was so dense, and she really just wanted to close her eyes and sleep. Harvey! Rayven forced herself to stay awake. She had to warn Harvey about that girl. Why was he sitting with her? Didn't he know how dangerous she was? She had to warn him. Had to push through the fog. The girl turned and looked at Rayven. It was like looking at herself. Harvey was suddenly no longer next to the girl. Instead, he was standing over Rayven, and she was in her room at Grand Meadow.

"Hey, sleepyhead. Not just me having a bad day, eh?" Harvey's tone was simultaneously teasing and caring. Rayven realized at that moment that he had the aura of an eternal grandfather. He soothed and calmed as though that was his sole purpose. She tried to respond, but her mouth felt like it was filled with cotton wool.

"Girl...Harv...table." That was all she could manage. In

her mind, it was, "Watch out for that girl Harvey. She broke the table." Of course, that wasn't what Harvey heard.

"I know, honey. I heard you had an accident with the table and then you got scared. It's okay, just rest now." Harvey stroked her forehead, willing her to sleep. Rayven, in contrast, was willing herself to stay awake, but darkness overwhelmed her again.

"She freaked out. It came out without her expecting it, and she overturned a glass table! She's becoming dangerous. They're going to take her soon. We need to do something." Caleb. Rayven was unsure how long she had been out again, but she recognized Caleb's voice. He was in her room and seemed to be talking on the phone. Was he talking about her? She didn't break the table, the girl did! Or did Caleb know that, and he meant the girl was dangerous? Rayven didn't dare open her eyes. If Caleb was on her side, that was fine, but she couldn't be sure. She couldn't be sure of anything anymore. "We are going to have to figure out how to achieve this, but it needs to end today! Someone's coming, I have to go."

The doorknob rattled, and Rayven heard the access control mechanism beep as an authorized card was held against it. It was the method of access to the patient's rooms. Each patient had a card that only opened their room, and staff cards accessed all the patients' rooms. Rayven wondered for a moment how Harvey had gotten into her room earlier.

"Caleb! What are you doing here?" It was Dr. Hewitt's voice. Rayven tried to keep her breathing low and calm, imitating sleep. She would learn a lot more if she could eavesdrop on their conversation.

"I was just checking on Rayven. I heard about what happened. I just wanted to check that she was okay."

"Well, your shift ended more than an hour ago, and she is receiving the best care possible, as you well know, so perhaps it's time for you to go." It wasn't a question. It was an instruction.

"What...what is going to happen to her?" Caleb sounded nervous.

"Whatever do you mean, Caleb?" Dr. Hewitt was perplexed. "You know that our patients often have setbacks. It's not uncommon for them to believe they are ready to go home when they are far from the point of recovery. There is hope for Rayven, of course, but she will need much more intensive care before we can consider releasing her."

"Like what? What sort of intensive care?" Caleb took the words right out of Rayven's mouth.

"Well, Caleb, you know that it would not be ethical for me to discuss that with you. After all, you are not qualified yet, and Rayven is not your patient." Caleb was not backing down.

"You've discussed other patients' treatment with me. What makes this case different?" Dr. Hewitt was silent for a moment, and Rayven wondered if she had missed him leaving the room. She willed Caleb to continue pressing for an answer. She needed to know what they had planned for her.

"Caleb, I would highly recommend that you keep in mind that I will be giving your professors a report on your progress. I would hate to be forced to tell them that you have become emotionally attached to a patient to the point that you are disrespecting senior staff members." Rayven almost gasped. She had never heard the tone that Dr. Hewitt was using. He was threatening Caleb! On the other hand, why was Caleb, so interested in her treatment?

"That's not the case, Dr. Hewitt, and you very well

know it. I am interested in Rayven's treatment from a professional perspective. I've never heard of a mental condition that gives a 120 pound woman enough strength to flip a glass table that weighs more than she does." He paused, "And I'm very interested in finding out how one would treat such a condition." They thought that she had broken the table. They didn't know about the girl. She was in the same office with Dr. Hewitt, how could he not have seen her? Now she was going to be treated for something she hadn't done.

"I will be sure to let you read her file when the treatment has been successful if your true intent is learning, Caleb, but until then, your shift is over, and you have no further reason to be here." The instruction was explicit. Rayven was exhausted from trying to focus on what they were saying through the fog. The bitter disappointment of hearing Dr. Hewitt says that she would not be leaving Grand Meadow weighed on her, too. She let her mind go and drifted back into the darkness.

Fingers of light pulled at Rayven's eyelids. She was moving. The wheels on the hospital bed squealed, and she opened her eyes to see florescent lights flashing past. She tried to lift a hand to shield her eyes from the glare, but she couldn't move. She tried to lift her head to see why her arms wouldn't move, and she couldn't even do that. Panic welled up in her, and she started to squirm in the bed. The sheet covering her fell to the floor and was left behind. Whoever was pushing her continued on without noticing.

"No, Rayven, don't struggle, it's okay." The bed stopped moving, and Dr. Hewitt's face appeared above her. He was wearing his comforting smile, and Rayven felt slightly better.

"What is going on? Where are you taking me, Dr.

Hewitt?" Her mouth still felt filled with cotton wool, but at least she was able to get something out that made sense.

"You are going to need a small operation, Rayven." The panic welled again. "Now it's nothing serious, but I believe that it will help you to heal faster so that you can go home. That's what you want, isn't it?" Rayven nodded slightly.

"What kind of operation?"

Dr. Hewitt smiled accommodatingly.

"I will explain everything to you as soon as we get to the operating room. Is that okay?" It wasn't really okay, but Rayven was certain she had little choice, so she moved her head slightly in agreement. When she did, a searing pain shot through her skull, and she remembered the injury she had sustained from the table. A surge of hope welled up in her as she wondered, for a moment; if that was the reason she needed an operation. If it was just to stitch up her head, then nothing bad could come from that. Dr. Hewitt seemed to recognize that she was in pain.

"Is that cut on your head painful, Rayven? I'm sorry about that. I'll be sure to have surgeons take care of it while you're under."

Under. The operation was not about the cut on her head then. It was something more. Rayven studied Dr. Hewitt's face as he stood over her. He smiled, and as he did, he became the girl. Rayven struggled against her restraints.

"Keep moving." The girl said, in Dr. Hewitt's voice. Then in her own, the wispy, barely audible voice Rayven recalled from before, "You let them give you the medication, Rayven. I told you not to. Why didn't you listen?" Rayven continued to struggle.

"Who are you? Why are you doing this? You turned that table over and hurt me, now they think I did it!" The girl's face continued to float over her, although the bed was now moving. She couldn't be moving with it. As they neared the emergency elevator at the end of the hallway, the bed started to slow down, and the girl's face began to change. Her eyes were no longer amber but black, and her skin became grey and sallow. Rayven struggled, desperately trying to get away. The girl opened her mouth and let out a piercing scream just as the elevator doors pinged to open. Rayven was enveloped by darkness.

Chapter Five

Her next point of awareness was feeling pressure against her back. Her head was pounding as she looked around.

"Rayven, don't panic, everything is okay. I'm getting you out of here." It was Caleb. He had lifted her off her hospital bed, which now stood on the pavement next to the car. The pressure on her back was him trying to push her into the back seat of his car. They were in the street outside Grand Meadow. Rayven had a vague recollection of the entrance when she had arrived there so long ago. Just beyond the hospital bed, on the threshold of the door, lay Dr. Hewitt.

There was blood trickling out of his nose. Rayven started to let out a scream of terror, and Caleb covered her mouth with his hand.

"He's not dead, Rayven. He's just unconscious. Please, you have to trust me; I am not here to hurt you." With that, Caleb removed his hand from her mouth and shut the rear car door. Rayven, breathing heavily, watched in silence as Caleb pushed the hospital bed away from the car.

He checked the street both ways, then looked up at the building, clearly trying to see if anyone had witnessed him knocking out an old man and bundling a young woman into his car.

Rayven wondered for a split second if she should run. On the one hand, she did want to get out of Grand Meadow, and she really did not want to have whatever operation Dr. Hewitt had intended for her. On the other hand, she had no idea whether Caleb was friend or foe, and he essentially kidnapped her. The streets were dark. There was actually no one around to help her if she decided to run.

"Here, drink this." Caleb handed her a small bottle of pink liquid. It was around the size of the miniature bottles of alcohol you get in hotel room fridges. There was no way in hell she was drinking that. She felt awful already. Her head was pounding, and she was still extremely groggy from the sedative, but that was better than being knocked out again by whatever was in that bottle. "It will make you feel better, Rayven, I promise. It's not going to knock you out again." She refused to take the bottle. Caleb sighed. "If we're going to make it out of this alive, you're going to have to learn to trust me.

He twisted the cap on the bottle, holding the steering wheel with his knees and took a sip. "Okay, if I am not unconscious in the next minute, can we agree that this stuff is safe for you to take?" Rayven looked at him, wide eyed, watching his throat to see if he really swallowed. He did. One minute. Two minutes. Three minutes passed, and Caleb was still conscious.

"What does it do?" Rayven asked tentatively.

"It wakes you up. It gets rid of all that crap they've been pumping into your system. The meds and all that and opens your mind to accept the truth."

"What's happening to me?" Rayven asked even though she wasn't sure she wanted to know.

"I'll explain soon enough, but basically, you are not seeing the world for what it really is, and this," he handed the rest of the bottle back to her, "will help clear things up for you."

Rayven had absolutely no idea what he was talking about. He sounded like he belonged back in Grand Meadow with the rest of the patients. She did want to rid her body of the medication, though, so she took the bottle from his hand and slowly twisted the cap. Caleb watched her in the rearview mirror as she sniffed the contents. It smelled like nothing. She held the bottle to her lips and downed the contents. It didn't taste like anything either. For all she knew, it was water. Maybe it was one of those placebo effect experiments, Rayven thought.

"Thank you for trusting me." He said it in a low voice, and as Rayven looked up at him, Harvey was sitting in the seat next to him.

"Harvey?" Rayven felt like she was having another vision again, but this time she wasn't so sure. Caleb didn't seem at all concerned that Harvey had suddenly appeared in the car next to him. Harvey wasn't alone, though. He was with the girl, or the girl was with him, she wasn't quite sure which. One minute Harvey was there, then there would be a buzzing sound, and the girl was sitting there instead. Despite the terror she had felt before, Rayven did not feel afraid. She didn't know if it was that pink stuff or what had changed, but she suddenly realized that the girl was not there to hurt her.

"I knew her...from before," Rayven said the words out loud, but she didn't know what they meant. "She did something." Caleb watched her in the mirror.

"Just relax and let it come back to you, Bren, don't worry. Just allow yourself to remember."

"Fire. She was in a fire with me." Rayven could see the flames licking at a building. She was standing outside, watching it burn, and the girl was inside. "Why is she inside the building? She'll burn. I have to save her." Rayven could feel the heat of the fire on her skin as she approached the burning building. Then, as she entered the doorway, she heard a thud behind her.

"Oh my... no! Why did she do it?" The girl had jumped, but before she did, she had plunged a knife into her own heart. "Why did you kill yourself?" At that moment, the building rumbled around her, and Rayven realized it was collapsing. She lunged forward to escape, but she was too late. An eternity of darkness overwhelmed her, and she felt her own heart stop. Back in the car, she looked up at Caleb. "Did I die?" Caleb didn't answer. "I thought she was being selfish. I thought she did it to hurt me because I hadn't gone in to save her, but she didn't. She was trying to save me."

Rayven felt like a curtain had been pulled back to reveal a whole new universe. This girl had been in her visions long before that day. She remembered that now. She had always appeared as a threat, as someone to be feared and to hate. It was all clear now, though.

"Who is she, Caleb? Or who was she?" He remained silent, threading the car along the highway as the sun started to rise in some unknown place to which they had driven overnight. "Who was I? It doesn't make sense." Rayven covered her face with her hands. "None of this makes any sense, Caleb. I died in that fire but... I'm alive."

Caleb spoke quietly. "It will all make sense soon, Rayven. I promise. Let's just get you somewhere safe." Rayven didn't know if she could feel safe anymore, no matter where she was. There was too much that she didn't know, both about Dr. Hewitt and Caleb, for her to really trust either of them. She watched Caleb as he drove. He seemed extremely tense. His jaw moved from side to side as he ground his teeth together. Rayven realized that she knew nothing about him. Worse still, what she did know was that he had been posing as an intern at Grand Meadow for months. Now he had kidnapped her and refused to tell her what was going on. As much as he claimed that he was trying to help her, she had no proof of that. Dr. Hewitt also said he wanted to help her, and he had been taking her to surgery! She wondered whether he had planned to perform some sort of lobotomy on her. She had to be grateful to Caleb for at least getting her away from that, but who was to say that she wasn't being taken into something worse now?

The vehicle slowed. They were entering what looked like a rather busy city center. Small shops lined the street. Rayven had never been there before, and nothing looked familiar to her. People shuffled along in crowds on the pavement on their way to work, school, or one of the other places "normal" people went, Rayven thought. When would she be one of them again? She watched as mothers pushed strollers down the pavement playing dodgems with women whose lives had taken a different route in their business suits with their noses in their cellphones.

Rayven had decided a long time ago that she was not a city girl. The traffic, hooting, smog, and general tension of the city did not sit well with her. Rural settings, on the other hand, nature and connections with the land, helped to nurture her. She felt at home seated barefoot in the grass. It was bad enough that she had essentially been kidnapped. She really hoped she wasn't going to be kept in some tiny apartment in the city. She had been stuck in

Grand Meadow for long enough, where the closest thing to nature was a crow that was sometimes real and sometimes not.

"Hewitt!" Caleb blurted it out, and Rayven followed his line of sight to a red Mazda behind them. Dr. Hewitt had followed them, and as they slowed in traffic, he had brought his car to a halt and was getting out. Caleb pulled up the handbrake and unlocked the car. "Stay here!" He commanded. Rayven's heart pounded as she watched the two men meet in the middle of the road. The windows were all closed, but she could hear Dr. Hewitt shouting.

"Caleb, just give Rayven back to me, and this will all be over. She needs treatment!"

"She does not need your type of treatment." With that, Caleb slid something metal out of his sleeve. Rayven struggled to see what it was, and as he raised it in the air to strike Dr. Hewitt, she realized it was a heavy wrench. The single blow knocked the older man to the road. Rayven saw a trickle of blood ooze from his ear as his head slumped to one side. People were getting out of their cars; others were honking. Rayven wanted to get out of the car too, but she was terrified that Caleb might attack her. The traffic had started moving again, and Caleb was back in the car. He tossed the wrench onto the seat beside him, and the tires of the vehicle spun as he accelerated to leave the scene.

Rayven looked back at the body in the road. He was dead, he had to be. Caleb had killed Dr. Hewitt.

Chapter Six

THEY HAD DRIVEN FOR ANOTHER FEW MILES IN SILENCE. Rayven was terrified. She was convinced that she was trapped in a car with a killer. She caught Caleb looking at her in the rearview mirror a few times. She avoided his gaze. Finally, he spoke.

"I'm sorry you had to see that. I had no choice." Rayven didn't look at him.

"Is he...do you think he's dead?"

Caleb sounded uncertain when he spoke. "I don't think so, probably just out cold, maybe a fractured skull. Don't worry about him now, okay? He wasn't a good guy, Rayven; eventually, you will realize that."

"How am I supposed to know who the good guy really is, Caleb?" Her voice was filled with venom and louder than she had intended. She could no longer control the fear that was building inside of her. It was leaking out, and she had an intense desire to open the car door and push herself out while the car was moving. She could run. Rayven thought she could escape Caleb, but she couldn't escape what was scaring her the most. Herself. After acknowledging the girl's real role in what she assumed was her past, Rayven suddenly felt like she had no idea who she really was. Everything that she thought she knew about herself now seemed untrue or part of a different world. How do you outrun yourself?

"I'm taking you to your sister's house, Rayven. You will be safe there."

Sister?

"Okay, now I know you're lying because I don't have any siblings, Caleb. I don't have a sister!"

He was calm in the face of her fury, not confused or perplexed. It almost seemed that he knew what she was going to say before she said it.

"I know it's confusing now, but you do have a sister, and you love her very much. You will know her when you see her." That sealed it for Rayven. Caleb was clearly out of his mind, and he was trying to make her think that she was the crazy one. She had to get away from him.

"Can we stop somewhere so that I can use the restroom?" She asked it in a quiet, resigned tone, hoping he would believe she had accepted what he was saying.

"We'll be at your sister's house soon, Rayven. It's not really safe to stop; can't you hold it for a few more miles?" He was constantly checking the road behind him, clearly concerned that they were being followed again.

"Caleb, we've been driving forever! Please?" She kept her tone reasonable, trying not to let her desperation creep through.

"Okay, I'll find somewhere." He reduced his speed and started scanning the stores and businesses that lined the road in yet another unknown place. This was more a town than a city, a lot less metropolitan and more to Rayven's liking. In her experience, people in small towns like this could be trusted a lot more than people in cities. She was going to need someone to trust.

A gas station loomed ahead with a diner attached to the side. Caleb put on his blinker and moved the vehicle into a parking space. He turned to her. "Please be as quick as you can. We need to get moving."

Rayven nodded her head and opened the car door. Standing up after having been seated for so long, combined with the remnants of the medication made her head swoon slightly. She ignored it and walked quickly toward the diner. She looked back at Caleb, and he had his head bowed, looking at something on his cell phone. The door chimed as she opened it, and Rayven scanned the small restaurant area. A waitress approached her, blonde ringlets, and a striped apron making her look like she'd stepped out of a 1950s musical. She had a kind face, although tired. Small lines around her puckered red lips gave away the fact that she had enjoyed more than one puff on a cigarette in the alley out back between serving tables. Rayven could picture the ring her red lipstick would leave around her cigarette butts and on coffee cups.

"Table for one, honey?" The waitress glanced behind Rayven, wondering if she had missed a small child clinging to her legs, perhaps. She took in Rayven's outfit, the light blue twin set looked like something a hospital patient would wear. Her auburn hair, although still in a ponytail, was falling loose. She looked "disheveled" for want of a better word, but the waitress was used to seeing people who had been on long road trips stopping in at the diner. Most weren't wearing scrubs, but who was she to question? As long as they paid their bill and left a tip, they could wear a pink tutu and booster shoes for all she cared.

"I've been kidnapped." The words hung in the air for a moment while the waitress processed their meaning.

"You...what do you mean?" The waitress glanced at the parking lot.

"The guy in the maroon Volvo has kidnapped me from the hospital I was in. He killed my doctor, and I need your help. Please!" The fear in Rayven's voice was palpable, and the woman eventually reacted. It was, hands down, one of the oddest things Rayven had ever had to say to a stranger before, but there was really no other way to convey the urgency. The woman could either believe her or think she was utterly insane and call the cops on her. Either way, she would get help.

"Come with me." The waitress led Rayven into the back area of the diner, where the food was prepared. A large man stood in front of a grill coated in fat and the residue of burgers long eaten. He stopped flipping the burger as the two women entered. The waitress ignored him, so Rayven did, too.

"In here." She was holding open the door to the walk-in fridge, "It's cold, but he won't look here. You won't be in here for long. We'll get the police." Rayven hesitated for a moment as the cold hit her. The waitress put her hand on her back, "It's okay, you'll be safe in here." Safe. Rayven didn't know what that was anymore.

As the heavy fridge door slammed shut, Rayven positioned herself behind a stack of boxes filled with frozen chips. Anyone entering wouldn't see her, but through a small gap, she could see out the glass door and make out an area of the front of the diner through the serving hatch. The man at the grill resumed flipping burgers as though strange young girls hid in their walk-in fridge every day. The front door chimed, and the waitress greeted someone.

"Table for one, sir?" Her voice was a little shaky, although anyone who hadn't spoken to her before may not notice.

"No," Caleb glanced around the restaurant, "I'm looking for the girl that just came in here, in the blue scrubs. Where is she?" Without hesitation, the waitress replied.

"Oh, she's using the restroom. Why don't you have a seat. I'll see where she is."

"I'll find her." Caleb tried to push past her.

"Oh no, there's only a ladies' restroom back there, you can't go in." She smiled sweetly, "I'll be back with her in just a minute."

Caleb exhaled, irritated. The waitress left him standing there and entered the kitchen area again. She stood, out of view of the serving hatch, and whispered to the man on the grill.

"Phone the cops. Tell them we have a girl here who says she's been kidnapped. Watch him. If he moves, shout."

The griller looked at her with an unchanged expression. "The cops are already here."

The waitress followed his gaze and saw a police car pulled up in front of the diner. A uniformed police officer got out with his hand resting on the holster of his weapon. From the passenger's seat, an older man in civilian clothing emerged. He had blood running down the side of his face, and he was ashen. He pointed through at Caleb from where he stood and said something to the police officer. Whatever he had said made the officer retrieve his gun from his holster and arm himself. Caleb either sensed something behind him or noticed the concerned glances of the few patrons seated at the diner counter. The policeman was speaking into his radio, arranging backup by the time Caleb ran into the back area of the restaurant. The waitress, in the process of trying to sneak Rayven out of the fridge and into another hiding place, saw him coming and stood in front of Rayven, shielding her with her body. She searched Caleb's hands with her eyes for any weapons.

"You're not taking her, just back off. The police are here." Rayven stood behind the woman watching Caleb. She didn't want someone else to get hurt because of her.

"Ma'am, this girl is coming off some medication, and she doesn't understand what is going on. That man out there is a risk to her safety, and I need to get her out of here, please step aside." The woman turned her head to look at Rayven. She was about to tell Caleb that they could just let the police sort the situation out when he reached out and grabbed her shoulder, throwing her to the floor. Rayven fled deeper into the back area of the diner, desperately seeking an exit to escape. Caleb followed.

"Rayven! Dammit, wait." Rayven spotted an emergency fire door and slammed her fist down on the handle. The fire alarm wailed, only adding to the chaos and confusion. She pushed the door open and felt a shove from behind her. In the few minutes it had taken for her to walk from his car and be hidden in the walk-in fridge, Caleb had covered the back exit with his vehicle. His rear door stood open, and he shoved Rayven into the car, shutting the door behind her. Within seconds, they were driving away from the diner. Caleb weaved the car out the opposite end of the parking lot, but there was only one road to get out of town. Rayven could hear sirens in the distance as the policeman's backup neared the diner. As Caleb steered the car onto the road that would take them away from there, Rayven spotted Dr. Hewitt standing at the back of one of the police cars. He was talking on his cell phone and waving a hand around while he did. She was glad he was alive, but she suddenly felt differently about him. She couldn't put her finger on what it was, but she felt like he was not someone she could trust anymore.

"I really wish you hadn't done that, Rayven." Caleb's voice was low, but the anger simmering in his tone was a little frightening.

"Well, what do you expect? You bundle me in this car, try to kill my doctor twice, tell me that I don't understand reality, but you won't tell what is actually happening! Oh, and you want to take me to a sister who, according to me, doesn't exist!" She was just raging now, unable to control the fear, panic, and confusion that were welling up inside her. "So please tell me, Caleb, how I should behave, because I really don't know!" The tears came in a flood, and Rayven slammed her head into the back of Caleb's driver seat and sobbed. He was silent. Rayven's sobs slowed, and she felt the car come to a stop. Caleb had pulled into a wooded area just outside of town. No one would be able to see them from the road there.

Rayven sat back in the seat and watched as Caleb got out of the car. He walked over to her door and opened it.

"Let's stretch our legs." Rayven waited.

If a strange man kidnaps you twice, then drives you to the woods and suggests you go for a walk, if you don't hesitate your fear response isn't working.

"Oh come on, Rayven. If I was going to hurt you, don't you think I would have done it by now? Hell, in order to save you, I have hurt everyone except you!"

Rayven got out of the car and looked around her. The trees formed a green canopy over their heads. A trail between the trees petered off at a point further than she could see. Caleb started walking. She stood for a moment, wondering if she should run again. This would be an ideal place to kill her and hide her body, and it really would not be too smart to go wandering off into the woods with a strange man. She really had little choice, though. She could stay put, and he could kill her anyway, or she could at least die, having stretched her legs a little. She started walking, all the while checking around her to see where she could escape onto the road if she saw a car passing. She calculated the odds that a car would be able to stop before hitting her if she just jumped in front of it. The odds weren't good, but it was an option

For a moment, she enjoyed the birdsong that rose up from the canopy of trees. It had been so long since she had heard a bird. She wondered if this was what prisoners felt like after having been released from a long prison term. It was like she was experiencing the world for the first time again. Sadly, considering the position she was in, she could also be experiencing it for the last time.

Caleb sensed her hesitation. "If you want to know what's really going on, I'll tell you." She followed him. Her desire to know was momentarily stronger than her will to live.

Chapter Seven

IF CALEB DIDN'T KNOW THAT RAYVEN WAS LAUGHING, HE would think she was crying. Honestly, he wasn't sure which was worse. He had told her the truth, at least the abbreviated version of the truth, and, in response, she had plunked herself down on a large rock nearby and begun to laugh hysterically. She looked up at him, still laughing, although less maniacally now, with tears streaming down her face.

"So let me get this straight." She hiccupped. "You want me to believe that the visions that put me in the hospital are not a result of any mental illness but rather me remembering another life that I lived...300 years ago?"

Caleb looked at her. "Yes." He gingerly sat down on the rock next to her. "Look, I realize it doesn't sound like it could be true, but that's only because you're thinking with the brain that today's society has given you. People don't believe in magic anymore, or reincarnation or anything else that is very real."

"Reincarnation?" She had stopped laughing now and looked at him.

"Yes, you died at that moment you remembered earlier. That fire. You were reincarnated into the life you live now." Rayven's face was pale.

"And the girl? Who is... was she?"

"Is... she is your sister. Her name is Morgan, and that's who I'm taking you to now."

"See, that can't be right because I saw her die, Caleb! In that vision, she stabbed herself in the heart, and she died." Caleb was shaking his head slowly.

"No she didn't, she survived."

"For 300 years?"

Caleb sighed and nodded his head again.

"Do you realize how ridiculous that sounds?"

"Well, you wanted to know, so now you know."

"Are you 300 years old too?"

Caleb laughed. "No. I'm...well in this life...I'm 24. I suspect that I was reincarnated too, though, but I haven't figured out my past life yet."

They remained in silence for a few minutes as Rayven struggled to take in the reality that she was being told was now what she had to live.

"How did you find me?" Rayven asked, still trying to understand his role in the whole twisted story.

"Morgan hired me to find you and bring you home."

"My 300 year old sister hired you?" Caleb stood up. There wasn't anything more he could share with her at that moment. The rest would have to be told when they were in a safe place.

"Yes, Rayven, she did. I realize this is a lot to take in. We have to get back on the road again, though. Will you please stop trying to run away now?"

"Are you being paid?" If this was just a job for him, then that meant that any concern or care he had shown for her had really only been him getting a job done.

"In a way, but not with money. Morgan is going to help me figure out my past. That's my payment, but only if I get you to her in one piece, and soon. So please, can we go now?"

Rayven stood up and started walking back down the tree lined path toward the car. She'd arrived there believing that she had been suffering from a mental illness. One that had caused her unbearable visions that had disrupted her life to such an extent that she could no longer function. Rayven had to be admitted to Grand Meadow. She was leaving this place with information that she had no idea what to do with. Rayven wasn't sure which reality was worse. She had thought he was bringing her here to kill her, but the torment he had just given her might have been worse than death.

"Get in the front. Put this on and pull the hood up." He handed her a white fleece hoodie style jacket. She didn't protest, pulling it on and tucking her hair into the hood. She sat in the front seat and put her seat belt on.

Caleb walked to the road before they pulled the car out and checked for any police cars. If they had been looking for them, they were long gone, it seemed. He drove out onto the road and turned right, headed away from the town they had been in.

"How much further?" Rayven asked.

"About 30 minutes. You can have a nap if you want. I'll wake you up when we get there." Despite her protestations that she was fine and didn't need sleep, Rayven dozed fitfully for the next half an hour. She would occasionally wake with a fright and take a moment to figure out where she was. Each time she did, the knowledge of what Caleb had told her came rushing back at her, and sleep seemed like a far better option than consciousness. She woke again as the car bounced onto a dirt road. The rocks under the tires caused the car to sway back and forth as they drove. She didn't really like the fact that the house she was being taken to be so rural, but she didn't really have a choice.

The rumbling ended as the road flattened out into sand sans rocks, and a large white farmhouse came into view. Although the property was probably a farm at some point in history, there was undoubtedly no agriculture of any kind going on at that time. There were only a few yards of open land between the house and an extremely dense forest that surrounded the back and sides of the home, cradling it like a child in its leafy bosom. It was both gloomy and comforting. Rayven longed for a day when things just looked one way, and she didn't always get conflicting impressions from everything. Constantly doubting herself was becoming exhausting.

"Is there anyone here?" Rayven asked.

The property looked completely empty. No cars stood out front. The front door was shut, as were all of the windows. She didn't see a single window blind twitch as they pulled up into the circular sand drive in front of the house.

"Oh, they're here." Caleb sounded very sure of himself.

"They?" Rayven had been under the impression that they were going to see her so-called sister.

"You're going to meet a few people today. They are all friends, and you don't have to worry about any of them. Morgan will probably join us a bit later."

Rayven stepped out of the car and gave a quick yelp of fright. The boy had come out of nowhere. He looked about thirteen. He had a wide, pale face and large brown eyes. His hair needed a trim, and his fringe hung in his eye. He looked from Rayven to Caleb.

"Hey, Jimmy!" The boy's face suddenly gained a little

animation as Caleb called his name. He made a wide berth around Rayven and hugged Caleb on the other side of the car.

"She looks just like her." The boy half whispered to Caleb. Rayven had little time to dwell on Jimmy's statement as, just as he had, people started appearing out of nowhere. In all, about 10 people stood in the front yard, where Rayven was sure no one had been before. They all varied in apparent ages, some young like Jimmy and others in their 20s and older. It was the most diversified assembly of families that Rayven had ever seen.

"Rayven! Welcome, I'm so glad you're here." Rayven was engulfed in a floral scent and billows of blonde hair before she had the chance to react. The woman pulled out of the hug and smiled widely at her. Rayven felt instantly drawn to a kindness in her face. "I'm Isabel. How was your trip?"

Rayven looked at Caleb, unsure of how much to say. "Um... interesting." Isabel laughed.

"Ah, a rather Caleb-esque trip then?" She winked at Caleb, who reddened slightly.

"We ran into some trouble." Isabel's pretty face clouded for a minute.

"You got it sorted, I trust? Nothing coming after you?" She glanced up the driveway as though 10 police cars may round the bend at any minute.

"We lost them. You know I would never lead them here." Isabel smiled at him and then turned to Rayven.

"Well, let's give you the grand tour and get you settled in." Isabel linked her arm with Rayven's, and together they walked toward the farmhouse. Rayven felt strangely comfortable with Isabel. There was something familiar about her. The others were less friendly. No one made her feel uncomfortable, as such, but she did get the distinct impression that she was being stared at. A lot. There was a lot of whispering going on around her too, which made her feel equally out of place.

The house was a converted farmhouse. The outside was still relatively original white wooden paneling and the cottage windows you would expect from a farmhouse, but the inside had been modernized. The bottom floor consisted of a living room, which was clearly the most used room in the house. There was no television, but in its place, a bookshelf lined the entire wall, and Rayven didn't think it would be possible to even squeeze another magazine onto the shelf. She was impressed by the quality of the furnishings and figured that someone in the house must be rather well off, considering the sprawling leather recliners dotted around the room. The sparkling kitchen was fitted with high end equipment, and a large island counter seemed to be another gathering point for the residents.

"We eat all of our meals together," Isabel said as she led Rayven into the dining room, which housed the most enormous dining room table she had ever seen. "It's fancy, but we are very relaxed. Our favorite family meal is home-made burgers and fries." Isabel laughed at the contrast of eating such a meal on a solid wood table, which shone like a mirror. "What's your favorite meal, Rayven?"

Rayven felt a little confused about being asked for information about her preferences. She hadn't had a choice in what she did, wore, or ate for so long that it felt as though she didn't have favorites anymore.

"I don't really know, to be honest." Her cheeks reddened. "Burgers are good." Isabel smiled at her, kindly.

"You'll have plenty of time to spread your wings here, Rayven." She placed her hands on each of Rayven's shoulders and looked deeply into her eyes. "You can be yourself now. It's safe to be who you are."

Rayven thought it a strange statement to make. If she were honest, after all, for her to be who she was, she would have to find out who that person was first. Perhaps sensing her unease, Isabel moved from touching her shoulders into a full embrace. Although she barely knew the woman, it didn't feel uncomfortable to be embraced by her.

"Let me show you your room." Isabel pulled out of the hug and linked her arm in Rayven's again as they ascended the stairs to the second level. "I won't show you everyone's rooms. As you get to know everyone, they can show you themselves."

The upper level had been converted from six large bedrooms to 12 individual rooms. By Rayven's count that meant every person had their own room. Isabel led her down the hallway past almost all the rooms until, just before a large door at the end of the hall; she turned left and opened a different door. The room was simple, with a single bed against the wall, but it was bright and filled with sunlight from a large window that overlooked the forest area on the side of the house. The walls were painted pale blue, and the comforter on the bed was an identical shade. The carpet was plush, and Rayven couldn't wait to sink her bare feet into it.

She realized as she looked at the bed, that she couldn't remember the last time she had slept in a regular bed. The hospital bed at Grand Meadow had been extremely uncomfortable. She also realized with embarrassment, as she looked at the built-in cupboard and chest of drawers, that she had no clothing. The clothes she had been wearing when she was checked into Grand Meadow had been laundered after she had been given the scrubs to put on. However, it still remained in a metal cabinet in her room there.

"So we figured you were about a size six and a medium

shirt is that right?" Rayven looked at Isabel in astonishment as she opened the hanging cupboard and revealed three pairs of jeans. They were all brand new with the tags still on them as well as and five plain t-shirts in different colors. "We weren't sure of your taste, so we just got some plain stuff for now. There are sneakers in the box," She pointed to a shoebox on the floor beside the cupboard, "and underwear and some toiletries in the drawer." Rayven was blown away. She hadn't felt so welcomed and valued in longer than she could remember.

"Are you getting settled?" Caleb leaned against the door frame, his height taking up almost all of it.

"Yes, I can't believe all the trouble that everyone has gone to…"

Rayven's voice trailed off. She suddenly felt terrible for not trusting Caleb. Something still niggled at her, though. This all seemed too perfect. Why would a group of complete strangers go to so much trouble for her? What did they want from her? Rayven had to still keep in mind that she had for all intents and purposes been kidnapped, and being brought to a beautiful house with kind people didn't really change that.

"Maybe you could freshen up and change. You must be sick of those scrubs. Afterward, meet me in the room at the end of the hall. We've got some practice to do."

"Okay?" Rayven's confusion was evident. Caleb smiled.

"I'll explain as soon as you're ready." With that, he headed down the hall, and Rayven heard what she assumed was the big, heavy door open with a creak and slam closed.

"The bathroom is just down the hall to the left. I'll leave you to it." Isabel smiled and walked toward the door. "I'm just downstairs if you need anything."

"Thank you for everything, Isabel." Rayven meant it, despite her growing unease at being in this picture perfect house.

"You're more than welcome." With that, she was gone, leaving Rayven to rifle through the belongings, which were apparently hers and get ready for whatever Caleb had planned.

The large door at the end of the hall creaked, and Caleb looked over to see Isabel peering into the room.

"Is she showering?" Caleb asked.

"Getting ready to, she'll probably be a little while still." Isabel shut the door behind her and strode over to Caleb, who was seated next to the window. "How much does she know?"

"Enough, for now. It's not like she believes me anyway."

"She will after this." Isabel waved her hands around the room.

"Well, she's either going to believe me or run away in terror." Caleb laughed dryly.

"Just go easy on her."

"She must be prepared to protect herself, Isabel. We don't have time to waste."

"I know, Caleb, but this is a lot already. She needs time to adjust to the idea of what her new reality is."

"Let's just see how today goes. Maybe once she starts doing it, it will all fit together, and Rayven will understand."

"I hope so."

Down the hallway, Rayven was toweling off after her shower. She felt rejuvenated. Having been confined in the car for essentially two days, paired with the fear and exertion of trying to escape, had left her feeling sticky and uncomfortable. She pulled on the brand new jeans, snapping off the tag with her hand, and marveled at the soft cotton of the light pink shirt she had chosen. She brushed her wet hair back into a ponytail and looked in the mirror. Her skin had a glow about it that she hadn't seen for a long time. She wondered if it was the medication they had her on at the hospital, or maybe it was just a lack of fresh air. She had been inside Grand Meadow for so long that she longed to stretch her legs and walk through the forest that surrounded the house. She hoped whatever Caleb had planned didn't take long.

Rayven padded down the hall to her room and tossed her scrubs in the small waste bin in the corner. She certainly wouldn't need those anymore. Pulling her room door closed, Rayven started toward the large door at the end of the hallway. She was just a few steps away when it creaked open, and Isabel appeared.

"Oh, hey! The clothes fit great. I'm so pleased." Isabel beamed.

"Yes, thank you again. Is Caleb in there?" Rayven nodded her head toward the room she had yet to enter.

"Yes, ready and waiting." Isabel smiled, patted Rayven on the shoulder, and whispered, "Good luck," before walking back down the long hallway, leaving Rayven wondering what exactly she needed luck for.

"Caleb?" Rayven's voice was hesitant. She let the door close behind her, and as it did with a thump, she jumped in fright and realized just how tense she was.

"Hey, Rayven, over here." The room was enormous. It was mainly a conservatory with three sides being glass. The ceiling, too, was a glass dome. Rayven had never seen anything like it. Caleb was beside her now, watching her marvel at the room. "Glass is a better conductor than brick and mortar." Rayven looked at him.

"Conductor of what?"

Caleb took a deep breath, realizing the time had come. "Do you remember the incident with the glass table in Dr. Hewitt's office?"

Rayven wondered if she could ever forget. "Yes, of course, that's what started all of this. Everyone thought I did it, but it was the...Morgan…" Rayven was suddenly confused by her own explanation. It had made complete sense at the time, but what she had been told about Morgan in the interim didn't fit with her intentionally trying to hurt Rayven.

"It wasn't Morgan that did it, Rayven. She manifested as a precursor to your power, showing itself."

"My power?"

Caleb was absolutely calm when he replied. This part of the explanation would require even more patience than the part about her being a reincarnation of a girl who died 300 years before. "The glass table flipped, right?"

"Yes."

"You weren't touching it, and neither was Morgan, right?" Rayven nodded her head slowly in response. "So how do you explain a table that weighed more than both of you put together, flipping and smashing on its own?"

"I can't explain it."

She couldn't explain it. It made no sense, just as most of what had happened in the last 48 hours made no sense.

"Well, I can." Caleb looked intensely serious. "You did it with your mind. That is part of your power. You can move things with your mind."

Rayven looked at him, waiting for him to tell her he was joking and crack up into fits of laughter. He didn't, and instead, a nervous giggle escaped her own mouth. "Caleb, that's ridiculous."

He wasn't laughing, though. He was more serious than she had ever seen him.

"Rayven, you need to accept this. I realize it's a lot to take in, but we don't have much time, and I need to know that you can defend yourself when the time comes."

"What? Defend myself? From who?" Rayven planted herself in the nearest chair, her head in her hands. The last two days had just been too much. As she sat and felt the confusion and fear build up inside her, a pot plant beside her shifted.

"Did you see that?" Caleb asked excitedly. "You made that plant move! The intensity of your emotion activated your power." Rayven actually had seen it. She considered that perhaps she had accidentally knocked it with her foot when she sat down, but she was nowhere near it. Rayven stared at the pot plant as though it might jump up and snap at her ankles. "Bren, you are more than capable of doing this. You just need to harness that emotion inside of you and let it out as the intention to move things."

"Really, Caleb? That's all I have to do is move things with my mind!" She was up and pacing around now. "This is insane, Caleb."

Crazy as it seemed, for the next hour, she worked with Caleb to try and get that pot plant to move again. She summoned up all the emotion she could, but it just wouldn't shift. Eventually, exhausted, she begged for a break.

"Okay, Rayven. I understand you're tired. Maybe that's why you're struggling to control it." He smiled at her, but it didn't reach his eyes this time. "You did well. We can try again in the morning. I'm sure Isabel will have dinner ready soon."

Rayven returned to her room. She was pretty sure that she had moved the plant with her mind, but why couldn't she do it again? Rayven was exhausted. She sat down on her bed, having closed the door behind her. Rayven really hoped that no one would come knocking again for a while. She needed time to take in what had taken place to her and what she had been told in the last two days. None of it made sense, and at the same time, it all made perfect sense. Rayven, for the first time, noticed a landline phone on the chest of drawers in her room. A telephone number flashed into her mind. It had happened to her while she was at Grand Meadow, too. Every time she had seen a phone there in Dr. Hewitt's office and in the reception, the number had flashed through her mind. When she thought about the number, she couldn't attach a name or a face to it, but she did feel an emotion. Longing. For some reason, that telephone number represented something to Rayven that she missed.

Rayven stared at the phone for another five minutes until she could take it no longer. She got up and walked over to the chest of drawers. She picked up the receiver and started to dial the number that had flashed in her mind so many times before. On the other side, in some unknown place, the phone rang. Rayven let it ring, wondering by the fifth ring if she should just put it down. Quite suddenly, the line connected, and a man's voice filled her ear.

"Hello?"

Rayven paused, breathing deeply, unsure whether to respond, or just slam the phone down.

"Hello?"

"Hello." Her voice was weak and uncertain. The man immediately responded.

"Rayven? Is that you? Where are you? I've been so worried!" Rayven felt like she knew the man's voice but couldn't assign a name to it as much as she tried. "Rayven? It's Uncle Sebastian."

"Uncle Sebastian." She repeated it, at first without

recognition. Then a picture flashed into her mind. An older man, maybe in his fifties. He had salt and pepper hair, which had once been dark. It was cut close to his head now though, an army cut. He was tall and strong and had an outdoor feeling about him like he was a farmer or an avid hiker. The image made Rayven feel at home and comfortable. It was a feeling she hadn't had for a long time.

"Rayven?"

She realized that she hadn't spoken for a while.

"Yes, Uncle Sebastian, it's Rayven. I'm sorry I didn't mean to make you worry. It... It was out of my control." She couldn't bring herself to say the word kidnapped, although that is precisely what Caleb had done. There was so much more to what he had done, though. He had also told her things that, although initially sounded ridiculous, the more she thought about it, the more she thought he might just be speaking a grain of truth.

"That's okay. Listen, just tell me where you are, and I'll come and get you."

Rayven thought it wouldn't be the worst thing to see the man. She didn't have to go anywhere with him if she didn't want to, after all. There was just one problem. She had no idea where she was.

Chapter Eight

THE LEAVES AND LOOSE BRANCHES CRUNCHED UNDERNEATH her new trainers as she walked between the trees. She'd decided it was best to stick to the forested area until she reached the road. No one had told her that she couldn't leave the house, but something still niggled at her that if they knew, they would try and stop her. She hadn't told them she was leaving. She'd padded down the stairs shortly after putting down the phone with Uncle Sebastian. She was expecting to have to explain herself, and she had been surprised when the living area and entry hall were empty. She had heard voices coming from the kitchen and realized that everyone was in there, probably preparing dinner. Rayven hesitated for a moment, wondering whether she should at least let Isabel know she was going out. Something held her back from doing so, though. It wasn't like she didn't plan on returning. She just wanted to see her Uncle Sebastian and let him know she was okay, then she could come back and learn more about what these people wanted her to know about herself. Maybe she could meet this Morgan person who claimed to be her sister. She knew that there was a lot more to be experienced in that house, and despite the truly unusual circumstances of the last few days, she hadn't been scared off. Isabel was lovely and had made her feel so welcome that Rayven would actually feel bad not going back.

There was something in her Uncle Sebastian' voice, though, that said she had to give him the chance to see she was okay. He sounded so desperate and scared. She really hadn't meant to worry anyone, and honestly, she didn't think he could blame her. She had no control over leaving Grand Meadow despite what he had been told. Which brought up another question: why would Dr. Hewitt have said to him that she had left of her own accord? Did he not want to worry her family? Or did he not want the police to get involved, which would very likely happen if he had phoned her uncle and told him that she had been kidnapped.

Yet another thing that made no sense in her current situation. Why hadn't Dr. Hewitt just called the police in the first place instead of coming to look for her himself? Surely that wasn't standard practice for a psychiatrist? She even suspected that the only reason Dr. Hewitt had been with the police at the diner was that someone in traffic had seen what had happened and called them. He certainly didn't seem too interested in communicating with them when she and Caleb had been pulling out of the parking lot. Plus, she had seen him standing behind his car. The feeling she got from him was not good. So what was he trying to hide by not calling the police?

Dusk lengthened the shadows of the trees, giving the forest a slightly creepy feeling that wasn't there when you looked at it from the outside. She was almost at the road, though, and she quickened her pace. Although Rayven could not give Uncle Sebastian a town name, she had described some of the landmarks she had seen as they had driven through in the moments she had been awake. He had been able to place her location. She had been amazed that he had been able to figure it out from her vague description, but he had seemed genuine, so she accepted that he knew where she was.

"Okay, it sounds like you are just outside of Westbury," he'd said. "If you head out back to the road, turn right, away from the direction you drove in, and about a half mile up the road, you'll enter a small town."

Rayven reached the road and turned right, walking as close to the tree line as she could. The road was quiet, but occasionally headlights would pass her. She considered that she probably should have left a note and wondered what Caleb and Isabel would do if they discovered she was gone. They would probably be going up to her room soon to call her down to dinner. She pictured Isabel knocking on the door with no answer and then cracking it open to find an empty room. Would she panic? Shout down to Caleb? Rayven had no idea what their reaction would be because she didn't yet understand their true intentions.

She got the feeling, however, considering all the effort they had gone to getting her there and preparing for her arrival, that they wouldn't take too kindly to her having left.

Rayven had never felt so torn. She had felt safe with Dr. Hewitt like he had her best interests at heart, but the operation he wanted to do and the feelings she got about him at the diner had changed that. Caleb was still an unknown factor to no small extent. Although Isabel had made her feel more comfortable, at the same time, she couldn't put her finger on why she didn't fully trust Caleb. Now she was walking into a third unknown. Uncles Sebastian. Every time she said his name or thought about him, she felt a little bit better, less uncertain, but in truth, she still had no idea whether he was friend or foe. She was sure she had a history with him and could only assume considering he called himself "Uncle" that he must be family of hers. Rayven just wished that everything could become clear and that she could feel safe somewhere. As she saw the lights of what she assumed was Westbury appearing; Rayven wondered if she would, ever again, feel safe. Darkness was falling fast, and she hoped that Uncle Sebastian would agree to give her a lift back to the house because she certainly didn't want to walk back through the forest in the dark.

Westbury could be described as a one horse town if people still used horses. Instead, there were two or three cars parked outside the ice cream shop that Uncle Sebastian had promised would be there. It seemed to be the social hub of what was clearly a tiny town. A few people were on the streets, but they all seemed to be heading back from work as they had that quick step of people whose supper waits. Rayven wondered if one of the cars belonged to Uncle Sebastian. She didn't recognize any of them.

Standing at the window, Rayven peered inside. There were hardly any customers. She noticed a mother sat with her two young children. One was covered in ice cream as he happily helped himself, while the other was being fed tiny mouthfuls by his mother. With each cold bite, the baby pulled his face and then immediately swallowed and opened his mouth for more. A young couple sat close together in a booth, sharing a strawberry milkshake with two straws. Rayven heard a car door open and then slam shut, and suddenly she was engulfed in an embrace.

"Rayven! Oh, I am so glad to see that you're safe!" Uncle Sebastian pulled away from the hug, still loosely gripping her shoulders, and studied her face. "What happened to your head?" Rayven had almost forgotten the cut from the glass table. She had tentatively brushed her hair earlier, but it was healing quickly, and she almost didn't feel any pain anymore.

"It's nothing, Uncle Sebastian. I just had an incident when I was at Grand Meadow. I'm fine now." He looked exactly like the image that had flashed in her mind, and Rayven realized that she must have real memories of this man. Despite the sudden physical contact and the close proximity he still maintained, she didn't feel uncomfortable. She felt something relax inside of her.

"Shall we go inside? We can share a banana split like the good old days. How does that sound?" He winked at her, and she suddenly felt despondent. He seemed to have beautiful memories of their time together, but she had none. What were the good old days? Were they really that good? Not wanting to give her emotional turmoil away just yet, Rayven smiled brightly.

"That sounds wonderful. Actually, I might not want to share, I'm starving!" Uncle Sebastian chuckled.

"Well, that's fabulous news, because I didn't really want to share either. Two banana splits it is!"

Rayven felt overcome by a feeling of camaraderie that you only get when you are with someone who truly knows you. The pitted feeling in her stomach started to subside slightly. Uncle Sebastian chose a booth on the emptier side of the shop and excused himself to order and pay for their banana splits at the counter. He returned to the booth and slid in across from Rayven.

"It'll be a few minutes."

"That's fine." Rayven smiled. "It's worth waiting for."

Uncle Sebastian' face darkened, and he lowered his voice. "What happened, Rayven? I got a call from Grand

Meadow saying that you had left without telling anyone where you were going." Rayven frowned at that. That wasn't right.

"No, I…" She struggled to find the words. "It wasn't by choice, Uncle Sebastian." He sat bolt upright in his seat.

"What are you trying to say? That you were kidnapped? By who?"

"No, I wasn't… Actually, I don't know what it was. I don't know if I was kidnapped or saved from something worse, but the last two days have been the most confusing of my life, and I really don't even know what to believe anymore."

"Two banana splits?"

Rayven jumped. She hadn't even seen the woman approach them. She placed the plates down on the table.

"Shout if you need anything else."

"Thank you." Uncle Sebastian called after her, clearly also taken aback by her sudden appearance.

They spent the next 30 minutes eating their banana splits, and, between bites, Rayven shared the events of the last two days. At times, Uncle Sebastian would look at her incredulously, clearly astonished at some of the things she was telling him. It seemed that he believed her. She knew very well how insane it all sounded. When she was finished, so was her banana split, and she pushed the plate to the side of the table. Uncle Sebastian looked at her in silence.

"Rayven, you are very special, and I don't know how much of what that Caleb guy told you is true, but there is no doubt that your brain does not work the same way everyone else's does. That's why you went to Grand Meadow in the first place." He paused and covered her hand with his. "Dr. Hewitt is the only person that can help you. He understands this stuff like no one else."

Rayven was shaking her head. "Dr. Hewitt is not what he seems to be, Uncle Sebastian. I can't tell you exactly what is wrong with him or his intentions, but I know that I can't trust him." She paused and inhaled deeply. "What operation was he taking me for? Why do I need an operation? I'm not sick, you said it yourself. My brain just works differently."

"That I don't know, Rayven, but I can tell you that I would trust Dr. Hewitt's medical opinion over some intern who essentially kidnapped you." Rayven was suddenly terrified that he was going to force her to go back to Grand Meadow. In her mind, she calculated the time it would take her to get to the door and escape onto the road. Uncle Sebastian had a car, and he could chase her down faster than she could run. If she could get into the forest, she could get away, though. She had basically told him where the house was as well, so regardless of whether she lost him in the forest, she would have to go back to the house eventually. Caleb and Isabel would probably be so angry with her for giving up their location. She felt a bit stuck now, to be honest.

"I'm not going to make you go back there if you don't want to." As though he had read her mind, he reassured her. "I promise. If you really don't think that Grand Meadow and Dr. Hewitt can help you, then let me try at least. I just want you to be safe. You cannot go back to that house, you have no idea who those people are or what they want with you." Something struck Rayven about what Uncle Sebastian had not reacted to when she had told him the story.

"When I told you about Morgan, that Caleb said I have a sister, you didn't react." Uncle Sebastian looked at her blankly. "You didn't pull your face like that was a lie.

Do I have a sister named Morgan?" Uncles Sebastian sat quietly for a minute, seemingly weighing his words.

"Honestly, Rayven, with your family's strange history, there is every possibility that it's true." Her breath caught in her throat. "I've never met this person you're referring to, but that doesn't mean she doesn't exist."

If she had hoped that Uncle Sebastian could shed some light on the reality of her existence, Rayven now feared he may have confused her even more. How was it possible that someone who had known her for her entire life could not know if she really had a sister or not? On the other hand, Rayven had to trust her gut, and it was telling her that she was safer with Uncle Sebastian than with Caleb or Dr. Hewitt. She decided at that point that she would leave with him. He was probably right about going back to the house. She had allowed herself to be convinced by Isabel's kindness and the instant connection she felt with her. Yet, when it came down to it, she really had no idea who any of those people were or what their intentions were. In almost the full day she had been there, she had yet to see her alleged sister. There had been no further mention of her. She knew that she couldn't trust Dr. Hewitt, and she definitely did not want to go back to Grand Meadow. She couldn't say for sure that Caleb and Isabel couldn't be trusted. Still, she didn't have enough information to make that decision, and really that was their own fault, as far as Rayven was concerned. If they hadn't been so secretive and just told her what she needed to know, she wouldn't still be sitting there with doubts.

Her Uncle Sebastian was her third option. She felt comfortable with him, and if he was family, then surely she should be able to trust him without question. After all, he had been so concerned about her that he had arranged to see her just to make sure that she was okay.

"Okay, I'll go with you," Rayven announced, and Uncle Sebastian smiled broadly.

"Thank you, Rayven, for trusting me. I'm sure that once you're in familiar surroundings, everything will start coming back to you."

Rayven really hoped that was true because, at that point, she felt utterly lost. He stood up and held out his hand to her. "Let's get going. It's not much of a drive to my house, but we've got a rather treacherous mountain road to negotiate, which is no fun in the dark."

Rayven had noticed as she walked into Westbury that the road had arched into quite a tough uphill, and she had caught a glimpse of fog covered peaks in the distance. Uncle Sebastian must live just past those mountains. As they got into his dark colored Sedan, Rayven paused for a minute, casting her eye around the parking lot and the road that led into Westbury. She wondered if Caleb and Isabel had been looking for her. Westbury would have been an apparent place to look, but perhaps Caleb had thought she would go back the way they had come instead of heading further out into the unknown. It could be that they had decided to wait until morning, thinking that maybe she had become lost in the woods. It was also entirely possible that they had not looked for her at all and that she was indeed free to come and go as she pleased, and they had no concern about her whereabouts. She somehow doubted that, though.

"Buckle up." Uncle Sebastian instructed, and Rayven had a sudden flashback. She was about 1o years old and sitting in the passenger seat of a car that a younger Uncle Sebastian was driving. He said the same words to her, and as he did, something in the back seat caught Rayven's eye. The girl she had come to know as Morgan was sitting in the back seat, looking straight at Rayven. It wasn't like her visions, though. This was more like a memory, but how could she remember being 10 and Morgan, if she really was her sister, was the same age she was in all of her visions? Uncle Sebastian had clearly said he had never met Morgan. What's more, here, Rayven was vividly remembering her sitting in the back of his car.

"Rayven, are you alright?" Uncle Sebastian had started the car's engine and was about to reverse when he noticed that all the blood had drained from his niece's face. Her eyes snapped back onto him from where she had been staring at the backseat, and she was suddenly back in the present moment.

"Oh yes," she laughed hesitantly, "I'm fine, sorry." She shook her head, trying to rid her mind of the thought that perhaps even Uncle Sebastian was not entirely honest with her.

He pulled out of the parking spot in front of the ice cream shop. He turned onto the road that would lead them out of Westbury. Rayven felt a twinge in her spine. Not again.

"Rayven." The voice was a whisper from behind her. It wasn't Uncle Sebastian. His eyes were firmly focused on the road ahead as they entered the promised curves of the mountain road. "Rayven." She sat dead still, terrified of the twinges in her spine that were now creeping their way up her back. "Rayven, you have to get out. You are not meant to be here. You need to go back." It was definitely Morgan's voice. Terrified, she slowly moved her head to look behind her and looked straight into Morgan's eyes. Her pupils were smoldering embers, and her mouth was moving, but nothing was coming out. The twinge was in her neck and moving fast.

"Now!" Morgan screamed, and as she did, Rayven felt a force leave her body. The energy hit Uncle Sebastian, and he swerved to the right. The car hit the barrier and screeched along, metal on metal for a few yards, until finally the vehicle came to a halt and toppled over the barrier onto its side and then rolled over onto its back. Rayven was dangling in the air. Uncle Sebastian was unconscious, breathing but bleeding from his nose. Rayven pressed the button to release her seat belt and toppled from her seat with a thud. "Run, Rayven, now!"

Rayven pushed open the car door and climbed out of the wreck. Although she had no basis for her belief, she felt that she had to listen to Morgan. She had tried to stop Rayven from being sedated; seemingly knowing that Dr. Hewitt planned to operate on her. Her power had caused this accident, and although she was sure Uncle Sebastian was going to be okay, she couldn't stay there. Rayven felt that her destiny was not in this car. Caleb knew more, and she would never be able to move on if she didn't find out what else was really going on. She did have some kind of power. It was real, and she had just witnessed it. Caleb seemed to be the only one who could tell her what it all meant. As frightened as she was, she had to go back to him and find out more.

She stood on the roadside for a moment, assessing herself for injuries that she may not immediately have felt due to the adrenalin. She seemed to be okay. Her shoulder ached slightly from landing on it after the seat belt had released, but other than that, she was fine, at least physically. She started walking, trying to calculate how far she would have to walk back to the house. It was at least three miles. The road was dark. Rural roads rarely had streetlights, and this one was no different despite the treacherous bends. For the first five minutes of her walk, the road was lined with mountain peaks on each side. She guessed that if it was light, she would see an enormous valley just beyond. The only thing she could see now was the slight silvery glint of the metal barrier as the moonlight caught it occasionally. It was this she followed for safety.

Rayven thought about the embers in Morgan's eyes, and as she did, she was suddenly back at the building that had been on fire. She was standing among the ruins, some still smoldering. She could see her own body lying among the rubble, lifeless. In the distance, Morgan stood watching. There was a patch of blood over her heart where Rayven had seen her stab herself, but the bloodied knife lay on the ground now, and Morgan was walking away. She was upright, and her stride was steady. She didn't stumble as someone dying from a self inflicted wound. It was as if it had never happened.

She was back on the mountain road and heard a voice calling from a distance. It sounded closer than it was because the mountains channeled the sound. "Rayven!" It was Uncle Sebastian, clearly now conscious and trying to find her. She quickened her pace and continued down the road. Away from his voice and toward the flickering lights of Westbury. Suddenly, she was a young child and running through a meadow, this time toward a voice calling her name. It was Morgan. She was the same age that Rayven had always seen her as, and she was crouching down, holding her arms open for Rayven to run into them.

Back on the mountain road, Rayven started running. The two realities began to merge for her, and she felt as though she were running down the dark path into Morgan's arms. She realized too late that she was no longer running in the soft grass of the meadow and lost her footing in the gravel. Rayven met the tar with her hands first, the skin grazing off, and then the side of her face hit the gravel. She lay there for a minute, trying to understand what had happened. The headlights of a car illuminated the road around her. She heard the tires crunching gravel close to her head. It couldn't be Uncle Sebastian. Couldn't be. There was no way he had gotten his car upright and moving on his own.

"Rayven, are you okay?" She lifted herself up and into Caleb's arms. "Slowly, slowly. Let's get you in the car."

Rayven didn't argue. This was where she needed to be for now. Regardless of whether she had all of the information, what she wanted right now or not. Rayven figured that sometimes in life, you had to just trust and go with your gut. He lowered her into the passenger seat and helped her with her seatbelt. She looked down at herself. Her palms were bleeding, and her new jeans were torn on one knee. Her face stung to high heaven, but she wasn't up to looking at it in the mirror right at that moment. "Don't touch your face. We'll get it cleaned up at the house." A tear rolled from her eye and onto her raw cheek. The pain of its sting was welcome. Rayven was finally feeling something.

"You need to call emergency services or something for my uncle." She could feel Caleb looking at her and then back at the road. "We had an accident."

"Damn, Rayven, you are having a rough time!" She thought he wanted to laugh, but he managed to hold it in. It was quite ridiculous, to be honest. At this point, she felt like if something could go wrong, it would. Caleb got onto his cellphone and placed an anonymous call to the local police station, telling them where to find the accident scene. Uncle Sebastian would get the help he needed. Hopefully, he would understand that she needed to find out what was really happening. Her fear was that he would tell the police that she had been kidnapped and send them to the house.

"It all fits into place all of a sudden. I understand

how everything fits together." Rayven said, and she really meant it. For the first time in longer than she could remember, she understood how her past, present, and visions fit together. "I'm never going to just be a normal person, am I?" Caleb was quiet for a while.

"You don't want to be normal, trust me. When you finally recognize the power you possess and your place in the world, you will realize that normal is beneath you."

Rayven snorted.

"I almost killed myself and my Uncle with my power, Caleb, and then I left him there!"

"You just need to learn how to control your power again, Rayven. With practice, you will get there. You're fine, your Uncle is fine. I'm sure he's insured. There's nothing for you to worry about."

"Why was Morgan so insistent that I get away from Uncle Sebastian? Is he up to something that I should be aware of?"

"No, I just think she knew that you were headed off course. If you had gone with him, your path would have changed. We need to keep you on track."

They pulled up to the house, and a few lights were still on. Isabel ran out to the car and put her hand over her mouth when the moonlight illuminated Rayven's face, which definitely didn't make her feel any better.

"What on earth?" She ushered Rayven out of the car and into the house. The next hour was spent picking loose pieces of gravel out of Rayven's cheek and dabbing it with disinfectant. "I'm so glad you're safe, Rayven. We were so worried about you."

"I'm sorry, Isabel. I...I was so confused." Isabel put her hand up to stop her.

"I know. It's a lot. I fully understand. I just wish you

had spoken to us before you left. I promise that you are safe here. I will not let anyone hurt you."

"Thank you, Isabel." She meant it. Things were a lot clearer now. "I think I could sleep for a year. I'm so exhausted."

Rayven and Isabel said good night, and Rayven made her way to her room, where she planned to sleep as long and as deeply as she could. As she neared her door, the door to the room opposite hers swung open, and Caleb appeared. He had just showered, and his hair was wet. Rayven felt odd as she noticed how the rivulets of water ran off his hair and down his neck.

"Oh, I didn't realize your room was just across the hall." Rayven wasn't sure whether she was happy or unhappy about the idea of his close proximity.

"Yep, this is me." He motioned to his room. "I just wanted to say good night and check..."

"That I'm not planning on running away in the night again?" She interjected, and Caleb laughed.

"No, actually, I just wanted to check that you were okay." He paused. "You are not a prisoner here, Rayven. You can come and go as you please. You are here because you are safe here, and I came looking for you tonight because I sensed that something was wrong."

"I'm glad you did. Honestly, I was heading back here anyway." He looked surprised.

"Really?"

"Yes, really. I know I've kind of been a pain in the ass the last few days, but I was really confused."

"I completely understand that."

"I'm not confused anymore, though. I know that this is where I need to be. I may still not be 100 percent sure of all the details, but I realize that this is my path."

Caleb smiled at her.

"I'm really glad. We only want what is best for you, I promise you that." Rayven yawned suddenly, and although she tried to stifle it, she was unsuccessful. "Anyway, I think we both need a good night's sleep." He started to close his door.

"Caleb," Rayven chewed her lip. "Earlier, you said something about keeping me on track. On track for what? What is all of this leading up to?" Caleb looked serious.

"That is a chat for the morning when we're both fresh and have some operating brain matter. Let's just say, there's no simple answer to that."

She really did not want to have to wait for answers again, but she also wasn't sure she really could take much more without sleep, and Caleb seemed to feel the same. She suddenly realized that she had spent a lot of their car trip sleeping and he hadn't. He'd probably been awake for almost 48 hours straight.

"Fair enough. I'll see you in the morning." She started to open her door and then turned back, "Caleb...thank you."

Caleb smiled tiredly, nodded, and closed his door. Rayven stood for a moment, staring at the shut door, wondering if he was already in bed and drifting off to sleep. Tomorrow she would know what the point of all of this was. Sliding between the fresh bed sheets that smelled of jasmine, Rayven appreciated how it felt to be in a real bed again. These were the simple pleasures of life, she thought. She switched off her bedside lamp and closed her eyes, succumbing to a night of deep, restful sleep.

Chapter Nine

Fingers of light poked their way through the curtains the next morning, needling at Rayven's eyelids before she was really ready to wake. She lay there for a while. Looking at the ceiling, thinking about how much her perception of reality had changed in just a few days. There were still memories that she wasn't sure what to do with. She was unsure whether certain events belonged to this life or the last. She was grateful, though, that she no longer felt as though she were going mad. There was really nothing wrong with her in the medical sense of the word. What was happening was not something Dr. Hewitt could fix with his operations or medicine.

Rayven knew that the visions and episodes she had been experiencing were simply the real Rayven trying to get out. It was just a symptom of her mind's battle to assimilate her two lives. Dr. Hewitt hadn't been too far off with his "two halves" theory, only she didn't need his medicine to sort it out. Honestly, she didn't really know what her fix was or if she even needed one, but she was okay with that, too.

Rayven felt more whole than she had ever been. She was in awe at how easily she had accepted that. One minute she had been quite happy to believe that she was mentally ill, and that was the reason why all of her memories were so patchy. She had such a poor sense of self, and the next, she understood it all as though she were flying overhead and looking at the bigger picture while it formed. Puzzle pieces floated around until they found their place and then just clicked in. She knew there was more coming today and also that there was a chance that she would feel less sure about herself later, but for now, she was Rayven. A magical, beautiful composition of past, present and future.

With that thought in mind, she hopped out of bed and prepared for the day. She studied her face in the mirror for a few minutes. The scraping on her cheek wasn't that bad. She had a few raw spots which would likely scab over in a few days, and there was a blue patch on her cheekbone where it had met the tar with a thud, but before long, it too would fade. She made her way downstairs, drawn by the chatter and laughter in the kitchen. That was what a kitchen should sound like, she thought. She rounded the corner and was greeted loudly by almost everyone in the room. She smiled brightly and took the seat that Isabel suggested.

"Chocolate chip pancakes?" Isabel asked. The smell from the frying pan was intoxicating.

"Yes, please! They smell absolutely delicious."

"They are," came a muffled response from Caleb near the end of the table, who was already working into a stack in front of him. He swallowed. "Sleep well?"

"Very well, thank you." Two steaming pancakes were placed on her plate, and she reached for the syrup, writing her name in the golden goop on her pancakes. The older lady next to her giggled.

"Is that so that no one steals them?" Rayven laughed back as she cut into her pancake. It was a celebration of knowing who she was.

The group ate happily, and then everyone helped clear up afterward. Rayven was impressed at the teamwork the group displayed. With such a large group, things could quickly get out of hand if a few decided to pull in the wrong direction. Everyone here really seemed to be on the same page, though she still wasn't sure exactly which page that was, it seemed like a good one. She thought that the group wasn't all that different from Grand Meadow. However, she would never share that comparison with the people in the house. Everyone here was a little bit odd, too, and didn't share much about themselves, but they all had one thing in common. There was something about each one of them that made them different so that they couldn't really fit into the outside world. The significant difference was that at Grand Meadow, everyone was trying to fix the people there, but here, their differences were celebrated. To be here, you had to be special, and no one was trying to get out. Indeed, she probably thought that there were people out in the world struggling to come to terms with their special gifts that need a place like this to be able to live their best lives. Rayven could only hope they would one day find their way here.

"Are you ready?" Caleb asked Rayven as though she should know what she was supposed to be ready for. She chuckled.

"I'm starting to think that the definition of the word 'ready' may be open to interpretation."

He shrugged with a wry smile. "Hey, don't shoot the messenger."

Somehow Rayven knew that whatever was about to happen would be in the large glass room they had been in the previous day, so she started up the stairs, and Caleb followed. It was literally one of the most beautiful rooms she had ever been in, Rayven realized when they entered. She hadn't been in the right frame of mind to acknowledge it the previous day, but it really did hold an aura of strength and vitality.

"You said the glass is a good conductor?" Caleb nodded.

"Of your power, yes. Powers flow more freely in a glass room than one is predominantly brick. You'll find most witches have a conservatory or greenhouse on their property." Rayven took in a quick breath at the word 'witches.' Caleb hadn't used that word before. She considered that perhaps it was just her own biases that made her think the term had a negative connotation, and really it all made sense. Women who have magical powers are called witches. That doesn't make them bad or even good. It just makes them witches. She set her judgment aside, but Caleb had noticed her flinch. "I kind of sprung that word on you."

Rayven gave a nervous smile, hoping she looked more confident than she was. She really didn't want to be the scared little weakling that she had presented to the world for the last three days. She wanted to be someone who could take this in her stride.

"It's not such a bad word. Witches are cool, right?"

"They are, and you are."

It sunk in.

"I'm a witch." Saying it somehow made it a little more real. She couldn't help, of course, but conjure an image of an old hag dressed in black with a pointy black hat, a wart on her nose, and a broom. Well, just as any occupation changes with the times, Rayven thought, her's could too and she guessed modern day witches wore denim jeans, trainers and pink shirts, She could live with that.

"Yes, you are a witch, and not just any witch, either." Rayven raised an eyebrow.

"There are levels of witches? Like witch rankings?" Caleb laughed at her description.

"I imagine you could call it that, yes." He motioned for her to sit with him near the window and proceeded to tell her the rest of her story. "You are one of three of the most powerful witches in the world. You and your two sisters. Morgan and Alaina."

Two sisters now? Rayven thought.

"Sorry," She interrupted him needing clarity, "you haven't mentioned another sister before?" As she said that, a memory appeared so vividly in her mind that she felt she may be living it.

She sat cross legged on the floor. She must have been around 12 years old. Opposite her sat Morgan, also cross legged. All three of them were in their pajamas. Beside her sat another girl who looked almost identical to her and Morgan except her hair was a little lighter.

"Try now, Bren," Morgan said encouragingly. Rayven saw herself lift her hands, and a wisp of white air appeared. It formed a tiny tornado, and Rayven controlled it with her hands, sending it across the room and up against a standing lamp that toppled over on impact. All three girls giggled. Alaina lifted her hand and sent a finger of light toward the lap stand. The finger curled around the lamp and gently picked it up until it was standing again.

"I couldn't do that earlier!" Rayven heard herself say.

"It's because we're together. When we're apart, we can still use our powers, but we are strongest when we're together." We are strongest when we're together. The words rang out in Rayven's head, echoing as though someone had shouted them into a canyon. That phrase could apply to so many areas of her life. She was strongest with her sisters, and then with Caleb and now, inside this house. Her strength was blooming among its residents. Perhaps strength and unity would always be inter-connected.

The image faded, and she was back in the glass room with Caleb. He was answering her question.

"They are both your blood sisters but from different lifetimes. You were all born to different reincarnations of your parents. Alaina wasn't living in the lifetime that you saw Morgan in. This lifetime is the only one in which all of you are incarnated together. That is why these things have started happening. You have now come of age, and the time has come."

The time for what? Rayven thought, and again, a memory materialized in response. This one, however, was less happy.

She was at the building that she had seen burn down. The one she now knew she had died in. The building was not yet on fire, but she could see Morgan in the same window she would eventually throw herself from. A man was standing behind her, and Rayven could hear herself screaming, trying to warn Morgan that he was there. Rayven wasn't even sure that the figure was really a man. He was extraordinarily tall, and his face was not really formed. It was almost a blur, Rayven thought. She watched the man lift his hands, and flames suddenly engulfed the entire building.

Rayven's heart was pounding as this memory faded, and she looked at Caleb.

"Who is the man?"

The blood drained from Caleb's face. "Which man?"

"The man that started the fire that killed me." Caleb

was quiet for a while, considering how to word what he would say next.

"His name is Zachariah. He is the eternal enemy of your bloodline and your trio of witches."

Rayven was back at the house, now lying dead on the ground, and her spirit was standing among the rubble, watching Morgan walk away.

"I will never allow the sisters to reassemble!" The voice was booming, and Rayven turned to find Zachariah looming over her. "No matter where you go. No matter which life you are in, I will find you all and destroy you!" Rayven's spirit was safe, he could only harm her body, but the fear his words created transcended time. In the glass room, sitting beside Caleb, Rayven began to shake. Quite suddenly, though, she felt a strange calmness wash over her. In her memory, she looked up at Zachariah, gazing straight into his blazing red eyes.

"Come and get us then."

Chapter Ten

She was back with Caleb, and although the previous day, pieces of the puzzle were already starting to fall into place, now, it was all absolutely clear. She understood exactly how each of her memories fit into place and what the reality of her life was. She understood Rayven. She turned to look at Caleb, and he recognized that something had changed in her eyes.

"Zachariah is after us, isn't he? He wants to destroy all three of us." Caleb nodded slowly.

"Yes. He knows that you are all now incarnate in this life together and that as soon as you are reunited, you will be unstoppable. He will do what it takes to stop that from happening." Rayven nodded. She knew now. She understood that everything that had been happening to her had been leading up to this point. Her hands felt different. She looked at them and realized that the scrapes from the previous night were disappearing in front of her eyes. Her hands tingled, and she felt compelled to move them.

She stood up and moved away from Caleb, afraid that she wouldn't be able to control it the first time, and she might hurt him. He watched her with curiosity. A single flower sat right in the center of the room, on the floor, as though it had been placed there for this very purpose. It seemed the safest option. A flower flying into someone's head would likely do less damage than a flower pot. Rayven motioned to the flower with her hands, and the white smoke began to move from her fingertips. This time, as she focused, she could control its intensity. It didn't turn into a tornado and strike things haphazardly. It very gently picked up the flower by its stem and lifted it up into the air. She turned toward Caleb, still holding the flower aloft with her power, and slowly, it glided through the air toward him. She stopped it just in front of his face, and he smiled broadly as he plucked it out of the air.

"Now that," he said, "is my type of flower delivery." They laughed together, overjoyed that she had reached this milestone so soon.

"What would happen if I decided not to embrace this? If I decided to just carry on trying to live a normal life and forget that any of this ever happened?" As the words came out of her mouth, she had no doubt that there was no way she could do that. She just wanted to understand what was at stake. Options are great to have, but they are not always necessary for you to feel free. Rayven was starting to learn that.

"The Universe would continually put you in situations where you would be confronted with your realities. Many good people would get hurt and, without the protective shield of the trio, you and your sisters would be wiped out by Zachariah."

"Wow, those are some great options." Her sarcasm was palpable. "So either I embrace being a witch and live this life that is so completely far removed from normality, or I get to run for the rest of my life and probably end up being killed by Zachariah anyway?" Caleb nodded slowly.

"Pretty much, yes."

"Can we destroy him? Zachariah?"

Caleb looked uncertain. "I don't see why not, but all three of you would have to work together. He would likely reincarnate in a different life again, but you could get rid of him in this reality... Probably." Rayven barked a half laugh.

"You don't sound very sure about that, Caleb!"

"None of this is an exact science, Rayven. Everything changes as the Universe does. A single stitch in the fabric of time can change everything, and I can only tell you what things are now."

Rayven considered this for a moment. For too long, she had lived with uncertainty. She hadn't known who she was or why she was having visions. Now things were suddenly so clear, and although there was a major element of danger involved, she knew that she had to try. Running would only bring her more misery. If there was a possibility that she and her sisters could destroy Zachariah, then they needed to try. Even if that meant it only solved their problems in this lifetime. Having control of her power made her feel far stronger than she had before. She now had a way of protecting herself, and she didn't have to suffer through visions anymore. Everyone searched for meaning in their lives, and she had just been given one on a silver platter. What higher purpose could anyone ask for but an opportunity to rid the Universe of a great source of evil? Zachariah would probably not be the last source of evil they would have to fight. Still, he was certainly significant enough to make a major difference.

"So when do I get to see Morgan? You said she was

coming here." Caleb looked down, and his unwillingness to make eye contact frightened Rayven. "What is it, Caleb?"

"We don't know where Morgan is Rayven. Alaina has also disappeared. We think they are on the run together, trying to escape Zachariah until the three of you can be reunited."

Terror rose up in Rayven. She had wasted so much time running away from her destiny. Her sisters probably thought she had abandoned them. "Morgan was supposed to arrive this morning, but since she was in your vision in the car yesterday, and she didn't arrive this morning, we think there's something wrong. Isabel is trying to track her using crystal mapping now."

"It's all my fault!" She cried. "If I hadn't spent so much time ruining your plans, Morgan would be here by now."

"Rayven, you can't blame yourself. Think about the transition that you have been through in the last few days. Anyone would find it difficult." He put his arms around her as she sobbed, then pulled back and cupped her face with his hands. "Look, Morgan is probably just being cautious, okay? We will find her and Alaina. I promise you."

I promise you.

At that moment, she was experiencing both a memory and the present time. It was Caleb standing before her, but he was also someone else, someone from her previous life. A man that she had thought she loved. Suddenly she realized where her mistrust of him had really come from. It wasn't from anything he had done, but from the memory, she had of this other man.

"You remind me of someone."

He nodded. "Who? Do you know?"

"Morgan told me a story. When she met me, she said that my soul reminded her of that man too."

Rayven's brow crumpled.

"Was it a man that I loved?"

"Yes. She said that you had died assuming that he had led Zachariah to you, but that wasn't true. He sacrificed himself to try and save you." Rayven acknowledged, now looking back.

"That's right. Why does he remind me so much of you, though?"

Caleb shrugged.

"I'm not sure. Morgan figured that maybe he and I had been ancestors in some lifetime. I don't have any memories of being in a lifetime with you and her. We're still working on getting back my past life memories, though."

"That's your payment."

She sounded a little wry. It was unfair of her, and she knew it. She couldn't grade Caleb's integrity by the fact that he was receiving assistance in exchange for his help.

Most people would have asked for far more than he had. Honestly, the trouble he had already gone to far exceeded any payment he was getting from her sister. He deserved to know about his past lives just as much as anyone. It was actually quite a sad thought that he had helped her so much in understanding her previous life. Still, he didn't have any information about his.

"Yes, in part. My real payment is that I get to reunite three people who are extremely important to the Universe and watch them be safe and happy."

Rayven gave a half smile. "Fair enough."

They sat in the glass room until early afternoon, chatting about the things that Rayven remembered and how Caleb had come to be involved with the group. He told her that he had been a pretty wild teenager, lost and searching for meaning in his life when he had met Isabel. He spoke about his mother passing away and how her death had hit him hard as a young man. He wanted to know if there was more beyond this life. He had struggled with the finality of death. Isabel had taught him about the things that hid behind the veil in the world. The things that most people never get to see. As he had slowly learned about reincarnations, past lives, magic, and the fight between good and evil, so much started to make sense for him.

Rayven's heart broke at the image of a young Caleb losing his mother and searching for meaning in the world. She considered that perhaps they weren't so different after all, except that she had lost herself and in finding herself, she had also found him. Caleb held the flower she had magically delivered to him in his hand as he spoke, and Rayven noticed that it had started to wilt as the hours wore on. At one point, she took the flower from him, intending to find a bin to throw it away in. It was dying. After all, its usefulness was fading. No one wanted to look at a wilted, dead flower. As she held it in her hand, though, the petals started to perk up, and, within minutes, it was as fresh as it had been hours before. She was astonished, of course, but Caleb had seen that done before, once on a larger scale, in a dying human. It represented the opportunity at the new life that she now knew to exist. Reincarnation. Perhaps it was even possible to be reincarnated without dying. Rayven felt that maybe that was what had happened to her. In Grand Meadow, she had felt close to spiritual death. She had felt hollow and as though she were lost in the world. Now, she was experiencing a new life. The promise of a future that, although frightening in some aspects, was mostly bright and beautiful.

They also discussed the very real possibility that they would have to go looking for Morgan and Alaina. This was something that Rayven looked forward to. In learning about their existence, she had started to feel a growing need to be with them. She acknowledged that she would likely always feel like she was missing something if they were not there. The strength and power that had been promised from their reunion was enticing. But just the same, her desire to have her sisters back in her life was about more than magic. They were pieces of her soul that needed to be put back in place. She was terrified that they were in danger and that her inability to trust in the last few days had increased that danger. Caleb assured her that they could look after themselves, though. He had never seen two people who were more attuned to what was happening around them.

Morgan, having lived so much longer than most other people, could sense changes in the Universe before anyone else understood them. He told Rayven that Morgan also struggled on occasion with being who she was. Although she had her sisters, they were not really like her. She longed to meet someone who could understand the intense loneliness of living for centuries. Watching so many people that you love die and often be reincarnated into lifetimes that didn't involve you. Rayven couldn't imagine that type of pain, and it made her long to hold her older sister and tell her that she was no longer alone, even if only for now. Rayven was interested in discovering that Morgan was not the only one of her kind in the world. It made sense, really. She couldn't be the only one. That knowledge made her look at the world very differently. Any time she would meet someone new in the future, she would likely wonder if they, too, were 300 years old.

As the sun was at its highest and the room was becoming rather too hot to sit in anymore, someone knocked on the door. It creaked, and Isabel's face appeared. She looked exhausted, and Rayven was immediately concerned about her.

"I think I found them." She said. Caleb and Rayven looked at each other, understanding that their new journey together had just begun.

Chapter Eleven

RAYVEN SAT WITH ISABEL FOR THE REST OF THE AFTERNOON as she used crystal mapping to make sure that she was getting a correct hit on Morgan and Alaina's location. Rayven had been fascinated to see how Isabel held the crystal, suspended on a string above a map of the state and surrounding areas. Rayven actually couldn't remember the last time she had seen a paper map, and it was clear the one that Isabel was using was very old. It was very fragile and torn at some of the folds. As Rayven looked at her, she wondered how many thousands of generations of witches in Isabel's line had used this same map to find lost loved ones or people they needed to save.

"I'm guessing this won't work with Google maps?" Rayven had cracked, trying to break the tension a little. Isabel had laughed, but she was subdued, not her usual bubbly self. "Are you okay? Why don't you take a break? You've been at this the whole day."

Isabel rubbed her eyes. "It takes a lot out of me, but I can't stop now. You know what is at stake."

Rayven nodded. She did understand now, and she

knew why Isabel felt she couldn't take a break. "It's not just finding Morgan and Alaina. I have to make sure that I give you and Caleb an exact location to minimize the risk for you." It was a huge weight on her, Rayven could see it. Isabel went back to work.

She held the crystal above the map, letting it hang loosely. For a moment, it was perfectly still, and then, ever so slightly, it started to spin. As it did, Isabel lowered the crystal toward the map. The spinning increased in speed until the crystal thumped itself down on a spot on the map. The same spot had several crosses drawn on it.

"That's the 10th time it has signaled there. I think it's fair to say that is where they are." Isabel gently moved the map so that they could both look at the area. It meant nothing to Rayven, as she didn't know their starting point, but it seemed pretty remote. It made sense that they would move away from people to minimize the risk to others. If Zachariah found them, a great fight would result, which would put innocent bystanders in harm's way. "I know there are some ancient caves out there. I wonder if they've gone into hiding there."

Rayven was fascinated by the practice of crystal mapping. "How do you do it? How does the crystal know what to look for?"

Isabel smiled at her interest.

"I tell it with my mind. I picture whoever I'm looking for, and because my power is oneness with the Earth, the crystal is part of the Earth, so it understands what I'm looking for. You could probably do it too, though."

It was a suggestion Rayven was eager to try. She took the crystal from Isabel's hands and stood over the map in the same way she had seen her do it. "Now, just clear your mind of everything else and focus only on what you seek to find."

Rayven closed her eyes and pictured Morgan as she had seen her in one of her happier memories. Sitting cross legged as they practiced their magic together. She felt the crystal start to spin. She opened her eyes and remained focused on Morgan. The crystal twirled faster.

"Now, slowly start to lower it toward the map," Isabel instructed. Within seconds, the crystal thumped down on the spot with ten cross marks on it. "Well, there we go, that seals it." Rayven smiled, amazed at how easy it was. "You are a natural, Bren. That was really fast."

Isabel suggested that Rayven go and get Caleb so that they could start planning. She first knocked on his bedroom door, and when there was no answer, she tried the glass room, which was empty. She padded downstairs and found a few people in the living room. Some were watching television, others reading books while still others were just sitting quietly with their own thoughts. Rayven felt sad that she hadn't yet adequately met many of these people. She would be heading off to find Morgan and Alaina soon, and she doubted that she would ever get the opportunity to correctly interact with them. Life is like that, though, she guessed. Not everyone is there to play a great role in life. Some are just there, in the background, playing a supporting role in the bigger picture. She did wonder about the younger ones, like Charlie. Where were his parents? Did they know he was here? Had they sent him here because they struggled to deal with his special gifts? Again, Rayven was struck by how similar in concept this place was to Grand Meadow.

"Hey, has anyone seen Caleb?"

"Oh, I think he's outside," one of the women replied. Thanking her, Rayven made her way to the front door. She didn't have to go far. Caleb was in the front yard, working on his car. He was bent over the engine. He looked up at her as he heard her footsteps and the door closing behind her.

"Everything okay?" She asked, concerned that their only vehicle may be faulty just when they needed it the most.

"Oh yeah. I'm just doing a general check, making sure that everything is in tip top shape. We don't need any surprises." He rose up out of the engine cavity and closed the hood with a bang, grabbing a rag nearby to wipe his greasy hands on.

"We've definitely got a location for them. We got 11 strikes in the same place, so it's pretty much a certainty." Caleb nodded.

"Good. Let me wash my hands, and I'll have a look. Then we can start planning."

Minutes later, Caleb, Isabel, and Rayven were poring over the map.

"I know exactly where that is. It's near the caves, right?" Caleb addressed the question to Isabel.

"Yes, I think they might be trying to draw him out there, away from everyone else."

"Can I ask a question?" Rayven was afraid it was a stupid question, but she had to know. She was learning about this new world, and there always seemed to be more questions than answers.

"Of course," Isabel said.

"If we can use crystal mapping to find Morgan and Alaina, can't Zachariah do the same?"

"Thankfully, no. Crystal mapping will only allow you to find someone toward whom you hold no ill intent. Good magic cannot participate in evil, so if the crystal senses that you are searching for someone to harm them, it will not allow you to find them." Rayven was relieved. She had had a sudden moment of panic as she imagined

Zachariah using precisely the same means to track her and her sisters.

"Okay, so no, we need to start planning," Caleb said. "Let's round up everyone and let them know it's time."

For the next hour, all the residents of the house sat in the living room and were assigned tasks. There were calls to be made to other friends who lived closer to where Morgan and Alaina were to guarantee that they were aware of what would be happening in case Caleb and Rayven needed support. They needed gear in case they had to camp while they hiked out to the caves.

Rayven had pictured a quick chat and then thought that they would jump in the car, but she had no idea how involved an exercise of this nature was. Everything had to be planned. Nothing could be left to chance. Caleb and an older man looked at the map and plotted out their route, identifying gas stations along the way and places they could safely stop if they needed to. Others sat on the landlines, having intertwining conversations with people across broad stretches of the land who would form their support system. Rayven hadn't been assigned a task, and, not for the first time, she felt a little lost. She decided to go up to her room and start packing her things.

She was a little sad to be leaving the house. The room had felt like a sanctuary the night before, and now, it was likely she would never sleep there again. She thought about the next person who would call this room home. Someone else out there would need a sanctuary one day, and Rayven hoped they found the same peace here that she had. She thought for a moment that the room could be compared to a particular lifetime. You only occupy it for a moment in time, and then you move on to allow the next soul to fill the space.

Isabel appeared in the doorway with a backpack.

"You're going to need something to put your stuff in." She smiled. Rayven hadn't even thought that far.

"Thank you. You think of everything."

"I'm really proud of you, Rayven." Isabel looked at her with an earnest expression. "None of this has been easy for you, but you have really just taken the bull by the horns. You are so brave." Rayven didn't feel brave. The closer it came to leaving, the more the butterflies in her stomach lurched around drunkenly. She somehow knew that when the time came, she would find the strength, but as she stood there, Rayven felt like an ant about to climb Mount Everest.

"You have been an absolute rock, Isabel. I cannot thank you enough for all of your efforts. You've really gone to so much trouble for me." She wrapped her arms around Isabel in a spontaneous hug. She'd gotten much better at receiving and displaying affection in the last few days. "I'm going to miss you so much." Rayven still marveled at how close she felt to Isabel, considering she had only known her for a few days. Now that she understood soul links and some of her past life, she wondered for a moment if she hadn't been close to Isabel in another lifetime. She realized that it was entirely possible and looked forward to enjoying more of her in this life.

"There will be no need to miss me."

Rayven frowned in confusion. "What do you mean?"

"Well, I've just got a few things to finish up around here, and then I will be joining you. You and sisters are heading into a major battle, and I want to help you to defeat Zachariah."

Something leaped inside Rayven. That was such astonishing news. She really felt as though she had more of her life to live with Isabel. Their paths would not end there.

Rayven was about to express her excitement to Isabel when the woman's face went pale.

"Isabel? What's wrong?" Isabel turned to face the doorway. She seemed to be listening or sensing something in the air. She turned back to Rayven with a look on her face that terrified her.

"They are here. They've come for you. Get ready to fight."

"What? Who?" She was unable to form proper phrases and could not understand what Isabel was trying to say. Then she heard a blood curdling scream come from downstairs. Caleb appeared in the doorway, out of breath, from taking the stairs two at a time. He, too, looked terrified. In fact, the only other time she had seen such an expression on his face was at the diner when he thought the police and Dr. Hewitt might take Rayven from him.

"We are under attack. Isabel, you know what to do. Rayven, stay with me. Use your powers if you can." Isabel immediately moved to the stairs, but Rayven felt frozen in place. Caleb grabbed her hand and pulled her with him. "We have to move, Rayven." She sprinted behind him to the downstairs level. "Everyone at a window, you know what to do. Don't panic, just keep them away from the house. If they get inside, we are done for." Even in her terror, Rayven marveled at how everyone seemed to know exactly what to do. Each of the windows and the door were covered by a resident of the house. Caleb took her with him, and they crouched in the hallway out of sight. "Do you think you can use your powers if someone comes through that door?" Rayven looked at her hands. She could feel the tingling. She felt sure that she could. Rayven just didn't know what force it would come out with, but in this case, she guessed the greater the force, the better. She just didn't want any of the residents of the house to get hurt in the process.

"Yes, I think so."

"Okay," His voice was low, "we need to keep these guys out of the house. The others will use their powers too, but you are the most powerful one here, so we need you." Rayven nodded, uncertain if she was really ready for this responsibility.

"Who is attacking us, Caleb? Is it Zachariah?" Caleb kept his eyes on the door as he answered.

"No, I think these guys were sent by your Uncle Sebastian. He might be under Zachariah's influence." Rayven stared at him in disbelief. That could not be possible, could it? Suddenly, it hit her. If Caleb was right and this was her Uncle Sebastian, she had been the one to give him their location. She had done it unintentionally, of course, but the truth remained that she had let their secret out. She couldn't and didn't want to believe that this could be possible.

"Why would you say that? Uncle Sebastian isn't involved in any of this? He was trying to keep me safe." Caleb put his finger up to his lips to indicate that she needed to be quiet. Rayven tried to focus on the matter at hand.

From the spot where they were crouched, they could see the front door and many of the front windows. A man dressed entirely in black appeared at one of the windows. The woman manning that window raised her hands, and the black figure was stunned for a moment. Without thinking, Rayven ran toward the window. Just as the man regained his senses and started to run at the window again, she lifted her hands and sent a wave of white smoke at him. It hit him square in the chest, and he flew backward, disappearing from sight. Other men, dressed identically, rushed up against other windows, and the residents and Rayven held them back.

She was exhausted but knew she couldn't back down. Just then, she heard an almighty crash of breaking glass, and Isabel screamed. Caleb was on the man in seconds and attacked him. They fought for what seemed like an eternity until Rayven saw her chance and cast her power in his direction. The man flew backward, out the broken window, and lay motionless on the far end of the lawn. Caleb cast a look outside to see the wounded men being dragged away by their still standing counterparts. They were retreating. He turned to Isabel. She was bleeding, the broken glass from the window embedded in her stomach. A low groan escaped her throat, and a small trickle of blood ran obscenely from the corner of her mouth and stained her skin.

"Just hold on, Isabel, we'll help you." He turned to the others. "We're going to need everyone over her to help Isabel."

Rayven was frozen again. She sat huddled in the corner, staring, and wide eyed, as blood pooled around Isabel.

Chapter Twelve

"Rayven." She continued to stare. "Rayven!" Caleb's tone was desperate. "You have to snap out of it, we need you."

Rayven scuttled over to Isabel on her hands and knees. She looked in her eyes and what she saw frightened her more than the blood. The spark that represented Isabel's lifeforce was fading. Her eyes were becoming dull. Lifeless.

"No, no, no!" She shouted, shaking Isabel's body, "Don't leave us. Stay with us, Isabel." Caleb pulled Rayven to her feet and told her to hold hands in a circle around Isabel with everyone else. She did as she was told. Caleb began to chant words that Rayven didn't understand.

"Everyone. Focus your power and thoughts on Isabel. Send her white, healing light." Rayven tried to focus, but she kept seeing Isabel's eyes becoming duller and duller with every second.

"This is not working." She broke away from the circle and fell to her knees beside Isabel. She had healed her own hands, and she had made that flower come back to life, so she should be able to do the same on a larger scale. The circle around her closed again, and everyone now focused their energies on her. Rayven held her hands together in a prayer like pose until she felt the tingling become a strong prickling feeling in her fingers. Then she held her hands over Isabel's wound, watching as the white light moved from her hands into Isabel's wound. As Rayven did this, she lost focus on anything except that action. She was sure the others were still there, but she felt as though she were floating on a cloud, just her and Isabel. Isabel's eyelids started to flutter, and she opened her eyes and looked at Rayven. A small smile formed on her lips. She seemed notably peaceful. Then she closed her eyes, and Rayven couldn't see her chest rising and falling anymore. She was back in the room. Caleb had his hand on her shoulder. She was unsure how much time had passed. It could have been minutes or hours.

"Rayven, she's gone." Rayven shook her head and pushed Caleb's hand off her shoulder.

"No, I can do this. I can heal her." She tried again, but her power was not even absorbed by Isabel's body this time. It bounced back at her, knocking her backward. Caleb caught her and held her as she started crying.

"It's okay, Rayven, it's okay." Caleb held her for what seemed like hours as she cried for Isabel and what she felt her role in her death had been.

"I can't do this, Caleb. I am not the right person to do this. I'm weak. My fear blocked my power, and I couldn't heal Isabel." She sobbed between words. She had gone from feeling like she could take on the world to feeling as though her entire life was a joke in just a few short moments. How could the Universe think that she was the right person to be part of the trio of the most powerful witches in the world? She couldn't even save one person, how could she be expected to stop Zachariah?

"Rayven," he was whispering in her ear, "you have to stop. These people depend on us. They cannot hear you doubting yourself like this."

She moved out of his embrace and looked around the room. It was chaos. People stood around aimlessly, some sobbing, some merely staring at her or Isabel. The seamless teamwork that had existed between this group before had been destroyed at the moment that Isabel left this world. Rayven knew she was making it worse but felt it completely unfair that she should not be allowed to grieve, too. Why should she have to hold these people together? Why was this her lot in life? She stood up and strode toward the stairs with Caleb following her.

Isabel was dead, and it was her fault. If she hadn't been so stupid and told her Uncle Sebastian where to find them, this would never have happened. How could someone be given the responsibility to save the world from an evil force like Zachariah when that same person couldn't be trusted to keep information secret? Clearly, the Universe had no idea what it was doing when it picked her to be part of the most powerful trio of witches. What good was it bringing a flower back to life if she couldn't bring a person back to life?

In her room, Rayven sat on her bed and looked at the bag that she and Isabel had packed together just minutes before. Tears welled up in her eyes. She was such a mess. She desperately just wanted to be normal. She didn't want these powers or the responsibility of belonging to some super witch trio. It was all rubbish. She should be able to have a normal life without feeling either completely mad or utterly out of control. What type of choice was that?

"She wouldn't want you to blame yourself, you know." Caleb was standing at her door.

"Are you speaking for the dead too now?" Her anger

was not for him. It was for those men who had no right to take the beautiful life they did and also for what they represented.

She would never be safe. Within a second, she could be the next dead body on the floor, blood pooling around her and the spark fading from her eyes. That was what Isabel's death represented. Her own mortality. She hadn't even started her journey to find her sisters or defeat Zachariah, and already, people were dying. Would Caleb be next? Would she be next? Maybe the Universe was just cruel enough to make her watch everyone she cared about die and leave her alive to suffer. She suddenly had a taste of what Morgan must feel like. How had she done this for 300 years?

"I knew Isabel well enough to know that she never would have expected you to save her. She knew the odds when she agreed to protect you and your sisters, Rayven. Death was no surprise to her."

Rayven's eyes shot daggers at him. Clearly, he couldn't really believe that Isabel would have simply accepted death? "Why do people have to die to protect us? It's just ridiculous, Caleb. Why does any of this have to happen?" Her anger was fading back into deep despair and sadness. Tears streamed down her face.

"It's just the way the Universe works, Rayven. It's the fabric of life. Good versus evil. It's the natural order, and you are part of that, whether you like it or not." He sat down beside her, so close that their arms brushed up against each other. Rayven turned to him.

"I'm scared, Caleb." Her eyes were filled with tears, and Caleb wanted to make everything better for her. He knew it was impossible. "I just want to be out of this situation. I'm not cut out for this. I think you've got the wrong person."

Caleb leaned in and kissed her forehead. She didn't pull away. It felt exactly right to have him so close to her. Maybe if he got closer, he would also realize that she was not the strong, brave person he thought she was.

"I know it's scary, Rayven. I get scared too, believe it or not." He pulled her into an embrace, and she settled against his chest. "I promise you that you are the right person for this. Look at how easily you adjusted to all of this…" he motioned around, "craziness! You are special." He cradled her face in his hands. "You must accept that it was Isabel's time. You will see her again. She will be reincarnated as we all are. Do you really think that the connection you had with her was an accident? You have found each other before, and you will find each other again."

They sat in silence for a little while. Rayven's tears dried, and she looked up at Caleb.

"Do you know what really scares me? It's not the danger, not the risk of dying or losing people I care about. I am terrified that one day I am not going to remember any of this." It had happened before, after all. She had completely forgotten who she was, where she fit into the Universe. When she was in Grand Meadow, she had no idea about any of this. She had believed she was sick.

"Listen to me, Rayven. I will never let you slip back into that. Never." He sounded so sure that Rayven wanted to believe that he could keep that promise. "No matter where you go, inside this mind, or in this Universe. I will find you and bring you back home."

He was home. That image entered Rayven's mind with no active thought. He was her home. Wherever he was, she felt real. He was the one who had brought her back from the abyss, time and time again. "I need to know that you believe me because we need to go now, and things are about to get scary."

Rayven met his gaze, feeding off his strength.

"I believe you." She had said those words before, to a soul that was so similar to his, in another lifetime. She had believed him then too. She believed him now.

The idea that she could connect with one soul across many lifetimes had been alien to her just a week ago. Now it seemed like the most natural concept. It was almost as though all of these concepts. Magic, reincarnation, soul connections; had always been a part of her, she had just never had the consciousness to realize it. Now that knowledge had been unlocked, and she felt as though she was waking up from a deep sleep. Understanding soul connections and reincarnation certainly made dealing with death a little easier. If you knew that moment of death, as brutal as it may be, was simply the moment for passing into another lifetime for that soul, could you really be sad for that person?

Rayven could still mourn the loss of Isabel's presence in her life, but she could accept it if it really was her time to move on. Perhaps her own actions had been destined to lead to Isabel's death, and that was all just part of the puzzle. It was a difficult thing to accept, and she still wished it had never happened. Still, it was easier to understand if it really all was predetermined.

Rayven also realized that she had been selfish to think only of her own grief. Caleb had known Isabel much longer and had a deeper connection with her than she had. The rest of the people in the house were also deeply mourning the loss of their protector. Yet Rayven had focused only on her own pain. She knew this was a human reaction, but it was one she would like to work on correcting. If she was going to be a valuable part of this new world she found herself in, she had to start to think about how her actions impacted others.

Perhaps that was the lesson in all this. She was still Rayven, but she was no longer just Rayven, the person, she was Rayven, the member of a community. That appointment came with great power and great responsibility. By dismissing either, she would only be making things more difficult for herself.

With this knowledge of soul connections in mind, she thought how sad it was that most people in the world simply passed each other by with little regard for the soul inside the person. People judged others by their appearance, which, she now realized, was simply a container that you happened to land in. You had no control over who you reincarnated as. Also, she could just as easily have been reincarnated as someone else rather than a member of a witch trio. That was determined by soul destiny, and that was something she had to embrace. She turned to Caleb.

"I'm sorry for your loss." His eyes quickly filled with tears. "I know that Isabel meant a lot to you too. She was the one who introduced you to this world. Your loss is just as great." They held each other for a moment, two souls connecting over loss and discovery until both had shed their tears for Isabel, and their cheeks were dry. Rayven stood up and held her hand out to Caleb. "Let's go save the world."

Chapter Thirteen

IT HAD BEEN A FAR SADDER FAREWELL THAN IT SHOULD HAVE
been. Caleb knew that he was basically leaving the rest of
the house residents without protection, but he had no
choice, and they knew it. He had called an old friend of
Isabel's and broke the news of her passing. She was also a
member of the network, and her power level had been
similar to Isabel's. She had agreed to come to the house
and help protect the members until he was able to make
another plan. The friend would also advise Isabel's blood
family of her passing, an unenviable task, but one that had
to be done. A story was created to explain her death
without introducing an outsider into the picture. They
would take care of the men who had killed Isabel themselves. An official investigation would dig up far too many
secrets that needed to stay hidden. Her death would be
deemed as accidental. Only the residents of the house
would know the truth.

Of course, there was also the task of Isabel's burial to
undertake. Rayven had taken a short walk through the
woods and picked flowers for her, laying the bunch on her

now covered body. It was one last act of care for the woman who had cared so much for others. That was all the time, she had to express her grief. She gathered her backpack before looking around her room for the last time and closing the door.

As she made her way down the hallway, Isabel's door was open just a crack, and Rayven peered in. Isabel's floral scent still filled the room, and it knocked Rayven back for a minute. Eventually, the smell would fade, and there would be no physical sign of the woman who had slept there. The map and the crystal lay on her chest of drawers. Exactly where they had left it just hours before when everything was still exciting, and fun and they had been planning their trip to find Alaina and Morgan. Rayven opened her backpack and carefully placed the old map on top with the crystal. She was concerned that Morgan and Alaina would move and they would have no way of knowing. She silently thanked Isabel for teaching her how to use the tools. The skill would, no doubt, come in handy.

She guessed that this was another part of the soul connection you had with people. The things they taught you could change reality long after they were gone. The skill that Isabel had taught Rayven could literally change the future of the world. Rayven smiled at the thought of Isabel's legacy. She would find someone to pass that skill onto one day, and with each new person who learned the art of crystal mapping, Isabel would continue to live on in this lifetime.

"Ready to go?" Caleb was already in the car when Rayven got in.

She tossed her bag in the back seat and got in the front. Rayven was thinking about the first time she had been in this car. She was the one being tossed in the back seat. So much had changed in such a short space of time.

"I guess so." Rayven half smiled.

"With all the chaos, the car hasn't been gassed up. we're going to have to do it on the way." Rayven nodded.

"I brought the map and crystal along, in case we need to recheck their location."

Caleb seemed impressed. "Great. Good thinking." He turned the key in the ignition, and the engine roared to life.

They turned right onto the tarred road, the same way she had walked to meet her Uncle Sebastian. She thought for a minute about what Caleb had said when they were under attack.

"Why did you think it was my Uncle Sebastian that had sent those guys, Caleb?"

He sighed, probably not in the greatest emotional place to deal with the question, but she needed to know. She also realized she would have to tell Caleb, at some stage, that she had been the one to lead Uncle Sebastian there. The present moment was not the right time, though. She knew he wouldn't blame her. She still blamed herself.

"It's just a feeling, Rayven. Isabel had a feeling about him too. It doesn't take much in this world for someone to be turned against a family member. He could be doing it for money. Maybe Zachariah is threatening him, we don't know, but if he were to show up again, I certainly wouldn't trust him." Rayven nodded. She had thought the days of her wondering who she could trust were over, but it seemed they might never be.

"Wouldn't it be nice if everyone was just straight up and there were no hidden agendas or secrets? Imagine if you could just trust people outright, without question."

"Yeah, that would be nice, but that's not the way the world works." Caleb sounded distracted. Rayven looked at him and then followed his gaze to see what was attracting his attention. He was looking in the rearview mirror. She swung around in her seat to see what he was looking at.

"Don't!" He grabbed her shoulder and firmly faced her forward again. "Don't look." There was a car behind them. A dark sedan with tinted windows held a decent distance behind them. Someone else looking at the scene would likely think that they were just two cars driving the same road, but Rayven didn't think that was the case, and clearly, neither did Caleb.

"Just stay calm." He said. "They pulled out onto the road as we passed, about a mile back. They are maintaining pace with us." To prove his theory, Caleb put his foot down on the gas pedal. The car matched their speed while maintaining the gap. He slowed down, they did the same. They were definitely being followed.

"Do you think it's the guys that killed Isabel?" She asked Caleb. She almost wanted him to say that he thought it was. Revenge had been on her mind from the moment Isabel's last breath had left her body. It wouldn't change anything, and it certainly wouldn't bring Isabel back, but it might make her feel a little less powerless. She couldn't save Isabel, but she could avenge her.

"I don't know. It's quite possible." He checked the fuel gauge and muttered under his breath. Rayven recognized the road they were on now. It was the same mountain road that she had been on the night before with Uncle Sebastian. It seemed less treacherous in the light of day. Only Rayven was concerned about getting into a high speed chase with these guys on a road like this. She could see Caleb was too, and their gas light had just come on, indicating that they were extremely low on fuel.

"How long do we have on the gas?" Rayven asked.

"A mile or two. There's a gas station just after this mountain road, but I don't want to stop with these guys following us." Suddenly their car swerved to the left. Caleb swore and looked at the steering wheel.

"What was that? Did you do that?"

Caleb shook his head. "No, I think it was them." The car swerved again, this time almost hitting the barrier. "They're using magic, Rayven. Someone in that car is using magic against us."

"Zachariah?"

"Or one of his cronies."

Rayven didn't ask permission before she did what she did. The rage that filled her was partially around Isabel's death, but it was also about her life. The normal life that she would never have as long as men in cars were chasing her and trying to kill her. She felt the tingling in her finger as she pressed down the button to open the passenger side window.

"What are you doing?" Caleb shouted in a panicked voice. She could barely hear him, though, the wind was already whipped around her head as she raised herself up and sat on the inside of the opened window, her body half outside the car. She hoped Caleb would keep the car steady. She couldn't hold on because she would need her hands for this. One jerk of the car would send her tumbling down the mountain. She allowed the rage to build up in her as far as possible and then waved her hands toward the dark sedan. The white light left her hand, and this time, it was not a wisp or a puff of smoke. It was a giant gust that hit their car and sent it spinning. The driver did his best to correct the spin. Still, it was out of his control, and the last view Rayven had of the car was as it crashed into the barrier, crumpling the front like a tin can, a puff of smoke rising from the engine. The road then dipped, and she could see them no longer.

Rayven lowered herself back into the car, wound up the window, and Caleb was laughing. He high fived her.

"Good job, Bren!"

She smiled, grateful that, at least, she had been able to save them if not Isabel. "Okay, we're almost in the next town. I'm going to pull over for gas."

"I think this is where Uncle Sebastian lives." Caleb looked at her.

"Why do you think that?"

"When I was in the car with him, he told me that his house was on the other side of the winding road."

The town came into view, and one of the first buildings on the main road was a gas station. Buckley's Gas and Grub, the neon sign proclaimed. Caleb slowed the car and put his blinker on.

"Okay. Well, we don't have a choice, we'll just have to be quick and keep our eyes open."

Rayven nodded. "You gas up, I'll keep watch." She had no idea where this new confidence was coming from. Still, she was feeling her panic and anxiety stripping away in layers to reveal what, perhaps, she had always been, a confident, strong young woman who was not afraid of who she was.

Caleb pulled up next to a pump, and they both got out of the car. Rayven watched as the dial ticked upward, and the gas pumped into the tank, willing it to go faster. Being an older town, the pumps didn't have card facilities on them, so Caleb would have to go inside the convenience store to pay. Finally, the pump clicked as the tank reached the brim. Caleb pulled the pump head out of the tank and closed the tank latch.

"I think you should come inside with me." Rayven nodded.

"I need to use the restroom quickly anyway." They

both scanned the parking lot before locking the car and heading toward the brightly painted building, which housed the gas station convenience store and restrooms. They got to the entrance, and Rayven started to move toward the restrooms.

"Wait, don't you want me to…"

"Come with me?" Rayven burst out laughing, and Caleb couldn't help but join in. The ridiculousness of the situation was clearly evident to them both. "No, I think I'll manage the restroom on my own. Thanks, though." He hesitated and then headed into the convenience store. She headed down a dimly lit corridor to the restrooms.

Gas station restrooms were never the best, but this one was one of the worst she had seen. She held her nose against the pungent smell of urine spilled in places it shouldn't have been and took longer than she should have to wipe every possible surface she had to touch. Eventually relieved both from a bursting bladder and simply just to get out of the smelly hovel, she used a piece of toilet paper to turn the handle on the door that led outside. The door opened on its own. She'd expected another gas station customer bursting in. Preparing themselves for the cleaning problem. Only what she saw instead stopped her in her tracks.

Chapter Fourteen

"UNCLE SEBASTIAN?" ALTHOUGH SHE DID HER BEST TO hide the uncertainty and terror in her voice, it leaked through into the air between them. He looked ragged. He had a goose egg lump on his head, which Rayven assumed was from the accident. She tried to get him to walk backward by walking toward him so that she could get out of the restroom, but he stood firm.

"You left me there, Rayven." His voice was filled with venom. Rayven swallowed. "I tried to help you, and you just left me in that wreck that you caused!" The last part of his statement was accompanied by a finger pointed into the middle of her chest. She staggered backward.

"I'm sorry, Uncle Sebastian. I was confused and scared. I needed to get back to Caleb."

His face crumpled into a sneer at the name.

"Caleb? Caleb?" He boomed, "You would leave your own flesh and blood, injured in an accident, to run back to some guy that you don't even know?" He was in a rage, and Rayven was suddenly terrified of him. He seemed genuinely hurt that she had abandoned him, but she felt like that wasn't the only thing behind his words. What he said next convinced her that this was not about the accident.

"I'm sorry about your friend." His tone was not apologetic, though. It was dull and emotionless, and everything that statement told Rayven hit her like a ton of bricks. He may as well have kicked her in the stomach. "She wasn't supposed to get hurt."

Suddenly, Rayven no longer felt bad for having left him in that crumpled car. Uncle or not, he was clearly not there to help her. "Why did you have to do that?" Rage bubbled up within her. "She didn't do anything to you! You had no right."

"I have every right. You cannot find your sisters. If you do, there will be no turning back." As he said this, he grabbed her arm and twisted it behind her back. She cried out in pain, and he put his hand over her mouth. She struggled against him, wondering if this was really going to be the place she died in. A filthy gas station restroom in Nowheresville. He was so much stronger than her physically. All she needed to do was get her hands free. She bit down on his hand, tasting blood as he screamed, and she was able to free herself. In her panic, she released some of her power but it only made Uncle Sebastian stagger back. It was enough for her to get out of the door, though. She scrambled up the passageway shouting Caleb's name. She could hear Uncles Sebastian' heavy footsteps not far behind her.

Caleb was at the car already and started to run towards her. Uncle Sebastian was right on her heels. Just then, a large yellow bus filled with school children pulled into the parking lot. They looked like they were headed out for a day trip somewhere. Rayven froze, and so did Sebastian. A slow smirk spread across his face. He knew that she would do anything to avoid those children from getting hurt. This would be his leverage.

"Rayven," Caleb called from behind her. "Just back up to the car."

"I wouldn't do that if I were you, Rayven," Sebastian called out. "You don't think that you're the only one with powers in this family, do you?" As he said that he raised his hands, and a bolt of fire shot out from his palm. The sign above him blistered, and two of the neon lights popped at the heat. A shard of glass exploding across the parking lot. Some of the children were already in the convenience store. Still, others were milling around the parking lot, and they screamed as the sign exploded.

"Get back on the bus!" Caleb screamed at them.

"Oh, yes, please, good idea, Caleb." Sebastian sneered. "Then, I can cook them all right in the bus like a tin of beans on a campfire." He raised his palm and pointed it toward the bus as children scurried inside it.

"No!" Rayven screamed and held her hands up, releasing a stream of white light. Sebastian moved his palm back to face her and released a strobe of fire at exactly the same time. The white light and the fire met instantaneously in the middle. Rayven and Sebastian stood firm, each pushing to have their magic win over the other.

Caleb held his breath as, at first, the fire receded, overcome by Rayven's light. Then the reverse happened, and Rayven was barely able to hold her position as the flames started to lick closer to her and the gas pumps behind her. She could not let those flames touch the gas pumps. If they did, everyone would undoubtedly die. She could handle her own death, and she could definitely handle her Uncle Sebastian' death, but she could not make sense of the deaths of innocent children. It was just too much, regardless of whether that was what the Universe had planned or not.

"I don't want to hurt you, Rayven! I just want you to come with me so that the Thorne link remains broken. That's all." Rayven was on the ground now, almost losing the ability to hold him at bay, and then he stopped. The bolt of fire receded back into his palm, and Rayven was left on the paving, gasping. Caleb ran over to her.

"Bren, are you okay?" She was gasping and nodding. "We need to get out of here."

Rayven shook her head. "No, Caleb. If we run now, this is never going to end. He will not stop. This ends today." Caleb recognized that she was not backing down. While he admired her courage, he had learned that some-times, you needed to pick your battles and, in this case, quite literally. Zachariah was their biggest problem. He didn't know that trying to defeat Sebastian was worth the risk of Rayven getting hurt.

"Rayven! You need to make your choice." Sebastian shouted from his position. "Come with me, and you save all of these little children." He motioned toward the bus where Rayven could see terrified faces pressed up against the window. The driver couldn't leave because half the children were in the convenience store, which had now been locked by the owner. He instructed the children in the store to huddle at the back where they would be safer if the glass front of the store came crashing down. Of course, none of these people could understand what was really happening. Witnesses would later say that a man had been wielding a blow torch. Although everyone present could clearly see that the flames were coming directly out of Sebastian' hands, their minds would not allow them to believe that. For those who had yet to be opened up to the possibility of magic, which was most of the world, they had to come up with a logical explanation that would sate their confusion.

"Rayven," Caleb looked into her eyes. "You have stronger power in you. You need to find it. You have powers that no one else does." Her brow furrowed.

"I don't know how, Caleb."

"You do, Rayven." He seemed so sure. "Morgan called it the Sealing Spell. She said it's the one type of magic that only you can do." Rayven looked into his eyes and felt something change within her. It had been a slow progression of recognition as, over the last few days, Caleb had introduced her to the person she really was. In some way, in his eyes, which spanned not only that moment but hundreds of years of love and commitment, Rayvenshe saw the final piece of the puzzle. She felt it click into place.

"Rayven! You're going to have to make a decision. Now. I can't wait around all day. What's it going to be?"

Rayven wondered when Sebastian had developed such a hatred for her. Had he also felt this way when they sat eating banana splits, and he had spoken about the good old days? She leaned in to whisper to Caleb.

"I have to be closer to do it." He looked panicked as she lifted herself up off the paving. "Stay here." She stood and faced Sebastian.

"Have you made your decision?" Sebastian asked.

"Yes," Rayven called across to him, "you've left me no choice." Sebastian took that to mean she was surrendering.

"Keep your hands behind your back!" Rayven complied. He knew she needed her hands for her magic. Or at least, he thought he knew. As she slowly walked toward him, her lips began to move in a silent chant. The words came to her without effort. Caleb had unlocked them.

Sebastian watched her lips moving. "What are you

doing? What are you saying?" She was thrilled at the panic she heard in his voice. She wanted him to be scared, just like Isabel was probably terrified in her last moments. A wind started to gust through the parking lot as Rayven continued to chant. It blew invisibly, a streak of white that began to circle around Sebastian' feet. He looked down at his feet and then at Rayven, his fear suddenly turning to horror as he realized what was happening to him. The wind continued to wind it's way up to his legs, leaving a cocoon in its wake. By the time Rayven was right in front of him, the chrysalis had encased him to waist height. He tried to lift his hands, but the wind was moving faster now as Rayven's chant increased speed, and struggle was pointless. Caleb watched in amazement. He had heard about this ancient spell but had never seen it practiced before. He was probably one of the few who had seen it happen in front of him. Such powerful magic is saved for only the most perilous situations, and Rayven had felt that the lives of 30 young children warranted it.

The cocoon had Sebastian fully encased now, and he was motionless. Rayven looked him in the eyes for a moment and then lifted her hands. She first aimed them at Sebastian and then slowly pointed toward the sky. In a white flash, Sebastian was gone. Rayven collapsed. Before she hit the ground, Caleb caught her. She was exhausted. As the children, simultaneously amazed and horrified, looked on, Caleb lifted Rayven into a fireman's hold and carried her to the car.

As he started to get into the driver's seat, he saw the gas store owner on the phone. The man was motioning hysterically. He must have been calling the cops. Caleb swore under his breath and started the engine. His tires screeched black tread marks on the paving as he pulled out onto the street. Rayven was out cold. He had no doubt that a spell of that magnitude would sap her of all her strength. She was amazing. He was so proud of her, and he knew Isabel and her sisters would be, too. He pulled his cellphone out of his pocket and dialed as he drove out of town.

"Hey," he said to the man on the other end of the line, "I'm about 10 minutes away from you, and I need another car. The one I'm in is probably all over police scanners by now. Can you help?"

"What the hell have you gotten yourself into now, Caleb?"

"Dad, please, I don't have time to explain. I haven't done anything bad, I'm just helping someone."

"Okay, you can take mine. I'll have it ready."

10 minutes later, Caleb pulled off the road and into a narrow farm lane. Childhood memories poured back as he jiggled over the stone road and stopped the car in front of a small cottage. True to his word, his father had the car started and ready to go. He had been cleaning the windscreen as they drove up.

"Hey, Pops." Caleb hugged his father tightly. "Thank you. I'll return it as soon as possible, I promise. You can use mine in the meantime." He gave a small laugh. "Just change the plates before you do." His father's years of hoarding would come to good use, as Caleb knew he had a whole pile of number plates that he had picked up off the side of the road throughout the years. Caleb had teased the old man throughout his life about the seemingly useless pile that just took up space. It had made no sense to Caleb that someone would need so many number plates that didn't belong to his vehicles. He was pretty sure that his father had not had this moment in mind when he had collected the highway remnants over the years, but he was glad he had done it. He would have to look past his father's hoarding habits in the future.

"What the hell!" His father had just spotted the unconscious girl in his front seat. "What is this?" Caleb laughed.

"Dad, it's fine. She's just exhausted. She's sleeping."

"Oh, thank heavens!" The old man gripped his chest. "I thought you'd kidnapped her or something." Caleb laughed again.

"Well, it was just the once, and it was for her own good." His father looked at him with shock. He really didn't have time to explain. The last thing he wanted was to lead the cops or, worse, Zachariah, to his father. "I'm kidding, Dad. Really I'm kidding."

His father didn't seem convinced but helped him transfer Rayven and the rest of the car's contents over to his car regardless. Although his son had seemed aimless in the past, in recent years, he had really got his life back on track, and he was proud of him. It certainly looked a little dodgy that he had an unconscious girl in his car and that he needed to switch cars. Still, he trusted his son when he said that he was trying to help someone and that he wasn't involved in anything bad. The men embraced, and Caleb thanked his father again before promising to return the car as soon as he could.

Soon they were off down the bumpy road again and back onto the tarred road that would lead them away from present danger and back into what was probably even worse danger. Caleb knew where he needed to go. He hoped that Morgan and Alaina were still in the caves. As soon as Rayven woke up, he would ask her to crystal map their location again, just to be sure. For now, he just wanted to get as far away from the gas station as possible. Gas! Oh, please be full, he thought. As he looked down at the gas gauge that pointed positively toward the big red F, he exhaled.

"Good old Dad." He hadn't realized he had said it out loud until Rayven started to stir.

"Hmmm?" She knew she had said something but wasn't quite sure what. Her eyes flickered open, and she immediately realized that a significant amount of time had passed. She sat up with a fright.

"Woah! Hey, it's okay. We're in the car." Rayven looked around.

"In which car? Whose car is this? Where's your car?" She turned to look at him. "Did you steal a car, Caleb?" The horrified look on her face was hilarious for some reason, and he started to laugh.

"No, Rayven, I did not steal a car!" He watched the horror on her face fade slightly. "It's my Dad's car. I stopped off at his place and swapped cars with him. The cops are going to be looking for mine."

"What happened? Back there, at the gas station. The last thing I remember was chanting and that wind that was circling up Sebastian' legs."

"You conjured the Sealing Spell, Rayven. Probably one of the most powerful spells in the Universe." Rayven looked at Caleb in disbelief.

"It was so weird. When I looked into your eyes, it was like," she struggled for the words, "you told me the words to chant."

"I don't know the words," Caleb said unbelievingly.

"No, it was like you unlocked something in me." Caleb smiled.

"Well, whatever it was, you were phenomenal. I was in awe of you back there." Rayven beamed with pride, and then a thought struck her.

"Wait, what does that mean? Did I kill him?" She panicked at the thought. Although he had been the reason that Isabel had lost her life, Rayven did not want to reduce herself to that level if she could help it.

"No, I think it just means that he's powerless now, trapped in that cocoon, for as long as you want him to be." Rayven nodded. "I'm sure Morgan will be able to tell us for sure when we find her."

Rayven looked in the back seat, reassured when she saw that he had indeed remembered to transfer her backpack.

"Speaking of which, I think we need to do another crystal map and see if Morgan and Alaina are still in the caves."

Rayven nodded. "I agree." She reached in the back to get the map and crystal.

"Do you want me to pull over?" She shook her head.

"No, I'm pretty sure I can do it while you're driving. Let's see how it goes. I'll let you know if I need you to stop."

For the next hour, while Caleb drove and late afternoon turned into night, Rayven tried to crystal map Morgan's location. She started with Morgan because she could more easily picture her. She had only seen Alaina in one memory. It wasn't working though, and she didn't know if it was because they were moving. She wished Isabel were there to explain. Eventually, frustrated, she asked Caleb to pull over.

"I don't know why it won't find her, Caleb. What if something has happened to her?" The panic in her voice was evident.

"I'm sure it doesn't mean that, Rayven." He slowed the vehicle and pulled onto the side of the road, leaving his hazard lights flashing to warn passing cars of his presence. "Try now."

She sat up straight and flattened the map on her lap,

holding the crystal in the air just above it, the way Isabel had shown her. She closed her eyes and focused on Morgan's face. The crystal hung limp. She tried again and again. Caleb breathed in.

"Okay, let's try Alaina."

"I don't know if I can. I've only seen her in one memory."

"You can do it, Rayven. Just focus. Try and recall that memory." She closed her eyes again and tried to recall the face of the third girl in her memory of her childhood. The face was so similar to hers that at first, she pictured herself. She shook her head and tried again. Eventually, the fog of her own face faded, and she was able to imagine Alaina. The crystal started to swing. She lowered it slowly, and it thumped down. Rayven put her finger in the place it had come down, and Caleb leaned over to see.

"No, that can't be right. Are you picturing Alaina or yourself?" Rayven looked at him with surprise. Was he reading her mind now?

"I did...picture myself to begin with, but when it started to swing, I was picturing Alaina."

"I think you should try again. That spot," he pointed to where her finger was, "is right here. Where we are parked right now." Rayven's heart sank. Obviously, that couldn't be right. She knew she couldn't do this. "You can't let your frustration get the better of you, Rayven. You need to focus. You can do it."

She tried again and got the same result. She tried countless more times, and every single time, the crystal thumped down right where they were parked.

"Okay, this is useless, we're wasting time." Rayven threw the map and the crystal in the back seat and put her seatbelt back on. "Let's go." Caleb paused for a minute and then switched off the interior light, preparing to pull off again.

Tap tap tap

They both jumped. Someone was outside the car, tapping on the window. Rayven raised her hands, preparing to arm herself.

"No, wait, Bren, it's me, Alaina!" Rayven and Caleb were both completely silent. They looked at each other, stunned beyond belief.

"Okay…" Caleb conceded. "I guess the crystal did know what it was talking about."

"Uh, is someone going to let me in?" Alaina asked. "It's pretty chilly out here."

Chapter Fifteen

AFTER THE SHOCK HAD WORN OFF, THEY DID EVENTUALLY let Alaina in.

"What the hell are you doing out here, Alaina?" Caleb asked. "Where's Morgan?" Alaina was shivering, and Caleb slipped out of his jacket and handed it to her. "Here, put this on."

"Morgan and I had to split up to confuse Zachariah. We figured that if we both stayed in the same place, it would be easier for him to find us. She stayed in the caves, and I walked out and hitched rides."

Rayven looked at this woman that she now knew to be her sister. She looked absolutely exhausted. She pictured her walking through the dark and cold with the knowledge that someone was after her and that Zachariah could appear at any time. It must have been a tough decision to split up. Rayven marveled at the sense of responsibility her sisters had displayed. Understandably, they had been working this much longer than she had. But to place their own safety at risk and suffer loneliness and fear to do what they saw needed to be done, took great courage.

Rayven knew that a new chapter of her learning had begun. Her sisters, one having lived many centuries of this life and the other having been aware far longer than Rayven, had so much knowledge to share with her. They could help to understand how she fits into this and what her role could be. They could teach her to hone her skills and learn new magic. Her powers might be even stronger than anyone knew, and with the right teachers, they could all be unstoppable. Her concern returned to her sister and the incredible journey she had been on.

"Alaina! That's so dangerous. You must be completely exhausted."

Alaina looked at Rayven with a small, tired smile. "Bren," She moved between the seats and embraced her sister. "I was so worried about you. I'm so glad you're here, and we're back together."

As Caleb drove through the night, Rayven and Alaina alternated between chatting and napping until daylight broke through the sky. Alaina had been horrified to hear that Rayven had barely escaped being operated on by Dr. Hewitt. Rayven learned from Alaina that the good doctor had been the downfall of many a witch. Especially those who had been put under his care due to the visions they had been experiencing. The girls would have known no better without having someone like Caleb to tell them the truth, and Alaina said that many had ended up having the operation, and they were never the same. Alaina said that she still wasn't sure if Dr. Hewitt was doing it on purpose or if he simply didn't understand how much damage he was doing. Rayven explained about him not calling the police when she was effectively kidnapped. Alaina took that to mean that he was possibly far more aware of what he was doing than they had realized. Dr. Hewitt could still be a problem in the future, and they would have to set up someone within Grand Meadow to watch him. After they had woken from one of several naps, Rayven realized that Caleb had been driving for a really long time.

"You need to have a break Caleb, you've been driving for too long." He stretched in his seat, holding the steering wheel with his knees. Rayven thought he was going to argue that he was fine and was surprised when he conceded.

"Yeah, I think I do need a couple of hours," he admitted. He slowed the vehicle down and pulled in behind a patch of trees that would shield their car from view. The girls got out, and Caleb got into the back seat. "Are you two going to be okay?" They looked at each other and laughed.

"Together?" Alaina smiled at her sister. "I would like to see anyone try us." Caleb laughed.

"Fair enough." Alaina's comment was indeed fair and not said with even a hint of arrogance. Rayven was still learning, but she was a powerful witch, and Alaina had her power paired with the knowledge of years of practice. Caleb actually would like to see someone try and take the girls on. He was sure it would be entirely entertaining. It felt a bit odd, if Caleb was honest, to have been Rayven's protector for so long. Even in Grand Meadow, when she wasn't even aware of it, and now she barely needed protection anymore. He acknowledged that he was certainly not useless to her, though. His role was simply shifting, and what she had said about him helping her to unlock the Sealing Spell made him think that there might just be more to their connection than he realized. He was excited to see what the future held for them.

Alaina and Rayven had napped enough during the drive and decided to take a walk to let Caleb get some rest without their chattering. They could hear water somewhere in the distance and started down a small path to find it. The river came into view quite quickly, and they found a large rock to sit on that overlooked the water. The early morning sun was still weak, but it was enough to have warmed the rock, so Alaina lay Caleb's jacket down on the rock, and they both sat on it. As they sat down, a tiny deer came out of the trees on the opposite river bank and started to drink. It was aware of Rayven and Alaina's presence but didn't seem bothered in the slightest by them. Rayven would come to learn that she and her sisters had a special connection to animals. She had loved animals throughout her life and had always had a knack with them. She had never thought that there was anything magical behind it, though. Once again, she acknowledged how much she still had to learn. It was also difficult to admit that she had lived much of her life with blinders on. She had only seen things for what they appeared to be on the surface for so long. Finding out about this whole new world was like having scales stripped from your eyes.

"How much has Caleb told you?" Alaina asked. Rayven considered the summary that Caleb had given her.

"I feel like he's told me my entire life story to be honest. Past lives, magical powers, Zachariah, Morgan being our older sister by 300 years," Alaina laughed at this, "oh and our Uncle tried to kill me." Alaina's face filled with horror.

"What? Uncle Sam tried to kill you?" It was Rayven's turn to look confused.

"No, who is Uncle Sam? Uncle Sebastian tried to kill me." Clearly, there was still quite a bit she didn't know and possibly yet another uncle with nefarious intentions on the loose.

"Oh, yeah, I would expect that of him. Uncle Sebastian isn't our real uncle. He tried that with me too. Morgan obviously knows everything about our history, and when I told her he was after me, she said he's not of our bloodline."

Rayven sighed. So many lies and so much confusion, she was so glad to finally be with someone who she could implicitly trust to tell her the truth. She thought back on how much time she had wasted feeling bad for hurting her own uncle. That lie had even led her to give up information that got Isabel killed. She wondered for a moment about how Sebastian' telephone number had become implanted in her memory. Could it have been done subliminally by Dr. Hewitt? He had phone Sebastian immediately after she had been taken from Grand Meadow, after all. It would make sense that they were working together. Sebastian has sung Dr. Hewitt's praises. Maybe he had even been the one to deliver her into his clutches. Rayven hoped that she would be able to figure out the connection in the future, and then maybe she could help save the future witches the pain that she had suffered.

It really made sense, though. Having her locked up at Grand Meadow and eventually operated on would be the perfect way for Sebastian to stop her from getting back together with her sisters. It all seemed to lead back to Zachariah, though. He was the ultimate puppet master.

"Well, good, then I don't feel so bad for wrapping him in a cocoon and sending him into the sky." Rayven laughed.

"You didn't?" Alaina's face was half amazement and half incredulity.

"I did." Rayven grinned, and Alaina grabbed her hand.

"You did the Sealing Spell on your own? That is amazing, Rayven! You're stronger than I thought." Rayven felt so proud. She really had found her place in the world. This was where she was supposed to be. "Morgan is going to freak out when she hears that!"

They sat there for an hour. Sometimes they chatted about what had happened and what the future held for them, and occasionally a comfortable silence fell over them. They just enjoyed each other's presence. Rayven felt it strange that it was possible to be so comfortable around someone who, although her sister, she hadn't even known existed just days before.

"I have something to show you," Alaina said. She reached into her pocket and pulled out her cell phone. She laid it on the rock between them and held her hand over it. White light started to flood from the phone, creating a beam that would have shot into the sky if Alaina hadn't stopped it in time.

"What's that?" Rayven asked in amazement.

"It's a power node. I figured out how to use my cell phone to make one. I had to shut it down because Zachariah could use the beam to track us."

"What does it do?"

"You can use it as a tracking beacon or amplify our powers. When all three of us are reunited, this will amplify our powers enough so that we can take down Zachariah."

"That's amazing!" Rayven exclaimed. Alaina beamed at her sister's appreciation. It felt so good to be back together.

They sat for another few minutes in silence, and then Rayven broached a topic that had been on her mind. She had asked Caleb the same question, but Alaina was looking at this from a totally different perspective.

"Alaina, do you think we will ever be able to live a normal life?"

Her sister gave her a half smile. "What's normal?" They laughed. "No, seriously, though, I think once we defeat Zachariah, we will pretty much be able to live whatever our normal is. We will always have to be close together, though, just in case. There is probably always going to be an enemy out there for us to take down." Rayven nodded solemnly.

"I get that." She smiled. "I guess that's the price you pay, right? For being the three most powerful witches in the world." They laughed at the description, although it was completely accurate. Alaina got up and stretched.

"Right," she said. "I think it's time we get sleepy head Caleb up and set out to Morgan. We've got work to do."

Rayven stood up and dusted off Caleb's jacket, which she folded and held close to her chest.

"About that." Alaina looked pointedly at Rayven.

"About the jacket?" Rayven joked, knowing full well what her sister was referring to.

"No," Alaina said in a teasing tone, "about you and Caleb." They started up the path. "Do I sense a bit of closeness between you two?" Rayven was quiet for a while, considering her response. She certainly respected Caleb and was extremely grateful for everything he had done for her. She would also concede that she felt a physical attraction to him, but she didn't want to confuse that for anything else. She didn't know how Caleb felt either, and he may see their bond as more of a brother/sister relationship than anything more than that. Rayven didn't even know that she would mind if he did feel that way. She really didn't have a good grasp on her own feelings at that moment. The last few days had been an emotional rollercoaster. Rayven almost didn't trust herself to put a name on what she was feeling or make any long term decisions based on her emotions. She had a long road ahead of her, and she really did want Caleb to be a part of that in whichever way the Universe intended. Her answer to

Alaina was less complex, and she hoped that none of her sisters had the ability to read minds in addition to their other powers.

"Well, we've been through a lot together in the last few days. I think it's only natural that we would have become close."

"Oh come on, Bren. It's more than that." Rayven shrugged her shoulders.

"Maybe, I don't know. That's not really important right now." She stopped walking and turned to her sister. "We have a life and death battle ahead of us, we can't let anything distract us."

"Including cute, dark haired interns?" Alaina teased as they neared the car. Rayven lowered her voice.

"Yes, including cute, dark haired interns."

Alaina was impressed with her little sister's emotional maturity. She had grown up so much, both physically and emotionally. She had apparently also grown significantly in her powers. She wondered with a tinge of excitement if she was destined to be the most powerful of them all. For now, Alaina was just grateful to be reunited with her, and soon they would be with Morgan too.

Thinking of Morgan made her anxious. She had hated leaving her sister in that cave alone, but they had no choice but to split up. She thought of the last time she had seen her. She had been standing at the mouth of the cave with a lantern in her hand. It had been the only source of light. They had thought about building a fire for warmth as well as light, but they were afraid that the smoke would give away their presence. Morgan had waved at Alaina after a tearful farewell and watched her until she was just a tiny dot on the horizon. Alaina had turned to look at her sister many times but eventually realized that she just needed to put her head down and walk. Hitchhiking had not been part of the initial plan, but a lovely elderly couple had stopped and offered her a ride, and by then, she was exhausted. She had gotten out at the next gas station and continued on from there. Her journey had been arduous, but she knew that, in reality, the real journey was just starting. She was grateful, at least, to be taking these steps with her sister and Caleb.

Caleb was waking up as they got to the car. He unfolded himself from the back seat and stretched, his shirt lifting slightly to expose a little strip of skin, and Rayven instinctively looked away. Alaina noticed but didn't want to make the situation uncomfortable.

"That was a good nap. I feel much better. Did you two enjoy your walk?"

"We did." Alaina said, "It was terrific to catch up."

"Okay, well, let's get going. Morgan is waiting for us, and then it's time to fight Zachariah."

Caleb got into the driver's seat and the girls into the passenger and back seats.

"Caleb," Alaina said, her tone suddenly serious, "I wanted to thank you."

"For what?" Caleb asked.

"For everything. For saving Rayven, for risking your life for us. You didn't have to do any of this, you could just drive off into the wild blue yonder and leave us here, you know?"

Caleb smiled and looked at Rayven and then Alaina.

"There is nowhere else I would rather be."

With that, he started the car and pulled back onto the road that would lead them to Morgan and, eventually, Zachariah and whatever waited beyond that. The car would only take them part of the way, and Caleb planned to park at an overnight truck stop and head out on their hike into the mountains from there. He didn't want to say it out loud, but he was concerned that the crystal was not picking up Morgan. It could be because she was alone in the sacred caves, but he wasn't sure about that. Even though she had lived for 300 years, that didn't mean she was invincible. It just means that the Universe had not decided that her time was up in this lifetime yet. When it did decide that, her age would mean nothing, and neither would her power or her sisters' powers. Zachariah was not out to just keep the girls apart. He was out to destroy them.

Chapter Sixteen

Rayven watched the mountainous landscape whizz by and considered all that she had come to understand since she had left Grand Meadow. She understood that not everyone in the world could be trusted, but she was grateful that at least she had three people she could trust. That was far more than many others had. She could not wait to see Morgan and learn from her sister. There was a knot in her stomach that she felt would only subside with her sister's embrace. She couldn't wait to ask her about the occasions that she had appeared to her in visions. Rayven had wondered how that worked. Was it some form of tele-portation or astral projection? Was it really her that she had seen, or was it just some sort of magical representation of her? The questions were endless, and she had no doubt that her sister had the answers. She would like to know more about her earlier life as well, the parts she couldn't remember. She wanted to know who the man that Caleb reminded her of was. Then find out whether they had loved each other before. She thought about how this hunt through time between them and Zachariah was like a game of reincarnation cat and mouse. He was this evil being who just drifted through time, waiting for the three most powerful witches in the world to be incarnated in the same lifetime. Then he started the hunt to stop them from reuniting. He had killed her once before, but her soul had gone on to be reincarnated. She wondered why he didn't just destroy her soul and be done with it. Perhaps he couldn't, or perhaps he chose not to. Some people just enjoyed the hunt.

She thought about Harvey suddenly and wondered if he was okay. She would love to be able to see him again. He had been so good to her when she was at Grand Meadow, and he had been so sad the last time she had seen him. She realized that he would only be getting Dr. Hewitt's version of what had happened, and that was painful to consider. Did he feel like he had lost someone he cared for all over again? The poor man had already lost so much. She had a wild idea that they could go and break him out of Grand Meadow, and he could live with them. He said his granddaughter was also special, so maybe he could quickly adapt to a magical life? She wanted to ask Morgan about his granddaughter too. Had she been a witch? Perhaps she had been reincarnated, and Rayven would be able to reunite them. She knew it was a pipe dream the moment that she thought it, though. They had far more serious matters to address before they could think about Harvey. Perhaps one day, though, she could see her old friend again. She sent a mental message out to him, telling him she was okay. She was pretty sure telepathy didn't work that way, but it was worth a try. Maybe he would be lying in his room, drugged up on whatever sedative they had him on, and suddenly see the thought pop into his mind? If it offered him a little comfort, it was worth the effort.

They were nearing the truck stop now, and Rayven knew that soon they would hitch the backpacks that were in the boot onto their backs and start the hike out to the sacred caves to find Morgan. Alaina had already done the walk twice, so there was no doubt she could show them the way. The thing that worried Rayven was what they would find when they got there.

She had told Alaina about Isabel and how she had tried to bring her back to life. Alaina had been confused, saying that they had never had power over life. When Rayven told her that she had been healing quicker than usual and that she had revitalized the flower just by holding it, her sister had been astounded. Not much more had been said about that topic because, although Rayven didn't know it, it was somewhat taboo. No witch had ever been given the power to bring people back to life. Forced reincarnations were actually considered more along the lines of black magic than white magic. Alaina was unsure what this meant about her sister. Was she some sort of new breed of witch? More powerful than anyone had ever seen before? The possibility was there, and perhaps Morgan would have some answers for them.

The truck stop loomed ahead, and Caleb put on his blinker to indicate his intention to pull in. They found a shaded spot near the 24 hour convenience store. Caleb hoped his dad's car would be safe there. The last thing he needed was for his dad's car to be stolen. That would not be a fun conversation. They piled out, and Rayven transferred the map and crystal to the hiking bag and then put her other backpack in the boot. When Alaina saw the map and crystal, she looked at Rayven in surprise.

"Did Isabel teach you that?"

Rayven nodded with a sad smile. "Yes. Just before she

died. It's how we knew that you and Morgan were in the caves."

"That's fantastic, Rayven. You really are developing in leaps and bounds." Rayven smiled, grateful for her sister's recognition.

Although the transformation from normal girl to powerful witch had been painful, as she sat with Caleb at her side and her sister just behind her. Rayven considered all that was ahead, she realized with satisfaction that there was nowhere else she would rather be either.

More Books by Renee

Jaeger Chronicles

Glen Cove

The Witch

The Djinn

The Countess

Magic of the Night

Raven Magic

Single

Tempest

Thank You...

Thank you for reading my book!
I really appreciate all of your feedback and I love to hear what you have to say. Please leave your review at your favorite retailer!